THE TESSERACT

THE SAGE CHRONICLES
by Karima Vargas Bushnell

Meet mysterious writer Halycon Sage, world-famous and possibly Native American founder of the Post-Modernist Minimalist Neo-Symbolist Pseudo-Realist School of Literature. (And read his collection of novels, measured not in pages, but in sentences.)

Book One
THE WAY BEYOND

Sage and No-Name Stupid, his TV-watching, motel-sleeping horse, have escaped into the western desert to save the world. They're helped by a brilliant but crazy Czech inventor, an Iraqi-American family facing ruin, Ruby—resourceful queen of the Dirty Dog Gang—and Ratbone of the Fifth St. Mofos. They're opposed by some detectives, some spies, and a shadowy figure of evil. The book critics, outlaws, and tiny invisible robots could go either way.

Book Two
THE BOOK OF SQUIDLY LIGHT

What's up with all those critics, immigrants, spies, and detectives, and who are these new space aliens and time travelers, not to mention the Apocalypse Zombie? Are the sparkly blue, telepathic, dimension-hopping

Squidren *friendly?* If a Cat Attorney and a beautiful Squidress fall in love, can it last? And what about UnVirtual Time Travel, LLC? What is *The Book of Lighted Squid* anyway, and does it hold the key to finally saving our planet for good?

Companion Anthology
SAGE'S MULTIVERSE MINI-SERIES

This unique collection explores a multiverse of ideas through its diverse range of storytelling forms. Encounter the Green World and the World of Light, increase your extraterrestrial knowledge with Five Tips for Intergalactic Diplomacy, accompany a bewildered writer as she navigates the chaotic world of airports, and meet a Cat Attorney who shares his diary and advises a canine inquirer on *dogagories*. So jump into a novel, a post or a poem. You never know where you'll come out, but you know it's going to be an awesome ride!

THE TESSERACT

Book Three of
THE SAGE CHRONICLES

Karima Vargas Bushnell

*The New Bestseller
That's Sweeping the Dimensions*

Delirious Walrus Publishing

Copyright © 2025
Written by Karima Vargas Bushnell

Paperback: 978-1-7334288-5-9
Ebook: 978-1-7334288-8-0

Library of Congress Control Number: 2025911619
Printed in the United States of America

Cover artist
Richard Ljoenes

Book designer
Pankaj Runthala

Edited by
Suzanne Bird-Harris
Chandi Lyn

PUBLISHER'S NOTE

To You
The Only One of You
There Is

GROWING REALIZATIONS AND ADVICE FOR THE HARD TIMES

AGE 10: The Romans were stupid to drink out of lead pipes and poison themselves.

AGE 30: They probably didn't know the lead pipes were poisonous.

AGE 50: They didn't have any other way to get water.

AGE 72: Our 111-year-old house has lead pipes.

*"If the end of the world has come
and you're holding a date palm shoot in your hand,
plant it."*

— Hadith of the Prophet Muhammad

peace be upon him

PREFACE

Taking an idea from the wonderful book *Flatland* by A. Square,[1] I've long felt that if my first book was a square and my second was a cube, then the third and final book in the trilogy, if there ever were one, must be a *tesseract*, a hyperdimensional supercube. I believe that without help from the Unseen, it could not have manifested as it has done.

The Sage Chronicles contain many complications and some apparent contradictions. When time travel, space travel, and travel between dimensions all happen at once, things can get complicated. Much of the series comes from personal experience and some parts of it come from illuminated wisdom—a gift, not an achievement. A few things come from ignorance, like the ideas about the Romans on the previous page, and for those I am sorry. This book concludes The Sage Chronicles, which began with *The Way Beyond* and continued with *The Book of Squidly Light*. The interdimensional alien *Squidren* have their faults, but you might enjoy or benefit from knowing

---

1 Schoolmaster Edwin Abbott Abbott, pub. 1884.

them. (The equally alien *Chilideans* and *Snrrrr* may be another matter.)

Several communities and cultures play powerful parts here, but it would be wrong to say too much. The world is full of such ridiculous humor, unspeakable beauty, and unbearable horror all at once, and we—the editorial we, not the royal we—have done our best to sketch that complexity here. Everything you need to know will be revealed, either in the short list below or in the book itself. Everything will be revealed. It always is.

EDITORS' NOTE: We've noticed that, throughout this text, there are annoying and unnecessary interpolations in the form of footnotes provided by some individuals calling themselves "the Mad Grammarians." We recall their superfluous presence in the previous volume, *The Book of Squidly Light*, where they added nothing of value except to clutter up the manuscript. Decisions regarding words and their usage should be left exclusively to the Squidren, who are obviously the sole experts in this matter. Thank you.

THINGS YOU'LL NEED
TO KNOW

If you don't mind a gradual unveiling or would rather be surprised when you read the first two books, you might want to skip the following. If you're someone who likes to know what's going on at all times, read on! It will be helpful to you.

The Way Beyond, The Book of Squidly Light,* and *Sage's Multiverse Mini-Series — Two novels and a related collection recounting some previous adventures, experiences, encounters, and insights from the cozy little multiverse you're about to enter.

Halycon Sage — Yes, our protagonist's name really is Halycon (pronounced HAL-i-cən). As explained in the early chapters of *The Way Beyond*, he didn't bother to look up the word when he first encountered it, and such laziness can lead to all sorts of problems.

<u>The Post-Modernist Minimalist Neo-Symbolist Pseudo-Realist School of Literature</u> — Sometimes snidely referred to by critics as "two-sentence novels," this possibly brilliant or possibly ridiculous literary innovation accidentally made Halycon Sage world-famous before the Event.

<u>The Event, the Great Event, or the End of the World</u> — In *The Way Beyond*, the literary and mystical Halycon Sage and the scientific Alexander Preisczech put their heads together to save our infinitely beautiful and precious Earth by destroying weapons technology. In *The Book of Squidly Light*, some well-meaning interdimensional aliens try to save it *again*, but their efforts lead to massive confusion (and some hilarity) and also to:

<u>The Splitting of the Multiverse</u> — "They had not realized that an intervention so massive would create a fork in the road, a splitting of the EarthWorld into one reality where the Great Event had occurred and another where it had not. The EarthWorld, perhaps not so significant in itself, had dragged most of the known universe with it when it split. There were now two of everything, at least in the part of the galaxy accessible to the appalled Squid team."

<u>The Alternate Universe</u> — The *rest* of existence (Earth, the galaxy, who knows?) which is going on exactly as it did before the massive interventions by Sage, Preisczech, Preisczech's Nanobots, and the Squidren.

<u>Dry Creek Gulch</u> — The part of Reality affected by the interventions above, apparently amounting to just one small and rather wonderful desert town and its immediate environs. People mostly can't get in or out, with a few exceptions, because of:

<u>The Wall, The Perimeter Wall, or The Barrier</u> — "Preisczech approached the peculiar barrier. Nothing could be seen except a faint shimmering in the air. But it was rock solid … besides the faint shimmer, there was nothing to be seen but the country beyond the wall, which was very similar to the country they had come from. Too similar … The thing was a *mirror.* Though it didn't reflect *themselves* at all, which made it kind of a funny one." Originally imposed by the Squidren, though they hotly deny imposing it now.

<u>Squid, Squidress, Squidren, Zi</u> — The masculine, feminine, plural, and gender-neutral nouns designating the Squidish race. The capital letter is essential, at least as we now understand it. "'Zi' was not always capitalized in the previous writings depending on how it was used. We are still investigating all these matters." — Sophie McGregor, Valedictorian Dry Creek Gulch High School

<u>SquidShip</u> — What the Squidren travel in. Its degree of physical reality apparently varies with the situation. We are still investigating. — Sophie McGregor

<u>The Nanobots</u> — Invented by Preisczech to take down nuclear weapons. After one Nanobot accidentally achieved consciousness through encountering a clothes dryer, this condition spread to the others. Excerpts from previous books tell us that they "wanted to go everywhere and do everything," but were, "not all that smart, if you want the truth."

<u>The Braided Thread</u> — A basic concept fundamental to Squidish culture and religion: That reality is made up of the Red, the Yellow, the Green, the Blue, and the Black, each standing for a range of qualities, capacities, and metaphysical concepts. Attempts to add other colors can be seen as shocking.

<u>The Braided Thread Teams</u> — Groups of beings organized according to their individual talents in line with the schematic above. In Book 2, aliens, humans, and animals came together in these teams to save the world.

<u>The Book of Squidly Light</u> vs. ***<u>The Book of Lighted Squid</u>*** — The name of this transcendental and metaphysical Squidish holy book is the main controversy within Squidish culture and has even led to wars. Read on to learn more.

<u>The Dirty Dog Bar a.k.a. the Canis Fidelis Grill and Juice Bar, or whatever it's called this week</u> — (The name changes a lot.) Originally headquarters and hangout of the Dirty Dog Boys, an old fashioned and relatively harmless street gang and opponents of the equally likeable Fifth Street Mofos, its name was changed by Anthony (Buzzard), who wanted a better atmosphere for the little Iraqi boy Nuri and his family.

<u>The Barbecue Incident</u> — The main argument for calling the holy book *The Book of Squidly Light* instead of *The Book of Lighted Squid!* The ambiguous second form could be misinterpreted, and *was*, by a supervillain, his minions, and some unwitting allies who, like the Nanobots, were not all that smart.

Welcome to our journey!

TABLE OF CONTENTS

Chapter 1 Far Future 1

Chapter 2 Far Future Again 7

Chapter 3 The In-Between Space 11

Chapter 4 Preisczech Explains 15

Chapter 5 In Dry Creek Gulch 21

Chapter 6 Preisczech Continues 29

Chapter 7 The History of Switching Up™ 33

Chapter 8 Dry Creek Gulch Again 41

Chapter 9 Concerning the Literary Conference 45

Chapter 10 Concerning Deandra 51

Chapter 11 Sage's Imaginary Author 59

Chapter 12 Halycon Sage Talks to Himself 63

Chapter 13 Meet Some Authors 69

Chapter 14 A Sip of Arabic 77

Chapter 15 Time Travel on Purpose 81

Chapter 16 Halycon Sage Talks to Himself Again 85

Chapter 17 A Peek at the Puppyverse 89

Chapter 18 The Other Side of an Old Friend 95

Chapter 19 Sometimes Arabic Lessons Can Hurt............ 99

Chapter 20 What's Truly Needed................................... 105

Chapter 21 Meet More Authors 111

Chapter 22 The Continuing Adventures of
              Edwin Puppy..................................... 117

Chapter 23 If You Expect Something Scary,
              It Might Actually Happen.................... 125

Chapter 24 Concerning Tiny Beings 129

Chapter 25 In the Court of the Multiverse.................... 135

Chapter 26 A Matter of Great Concern 139

Chapter 27 An Unexpected Setback.............................. 145

Chapter 28 Edwin Puppy in Dry Creek Gulch 149

Chapter 29 "Everybody Who's Anybody"...................... 153

Chapter 30 A Minor Annoyance 157

Chapter 31 The Science or the Puppy? 163

Chapter 32 The Science 167

Chapter 33 A Puppy in the House of Cats
              (with Interruption by Halycon Sage) 173

Chapter 34 Preisczech Explains Again............................ 179

Chapter 35 Rounding Up the Crew............................... 183

Chapter 36 Ruby Takes Charge 193

Chapter 37 "Go Get Them, Tiger"................................ 195

Chapter 38 The Concluding Adventures of
              Lawyer Puppy 199

Chapter 39 An Abrupt Left Turn.................................... 205

Chapter 40 The Program 213

Chapter 41 The Readings Begin.................................. 217

Chapter 42 The Readings Continue.............................. 223

Chapter 43 A Minor Panic 231

Chapter 44 Deandra Reads.. 233

Chapter 45 In the Court of the Multiverse, Part Two ... 243

Chapter 46 Some Special Information 249

Chapter 47 What Happened on the SquidShip............. 253

Chapter 48 The Real Defendant 263

Chapter 49 Back on the SquidShip 271

Chapter 50 A While Later 275

Chapter 51 An Intervention...................................... 279

Chapter 52 Chaos in the Court and What Followed..... 285

Chapter 53 A Triumph! 289

Chapter 54 Return.. 291

Chapter 55 The Beginning.. 295

CHAPTER ONE

FAR FUTURE

Dateline: 1.1.1212 S.R.H.H.
(Squid Robot Human Horse)

Olivia Squidlight was trying to get some writing done, but as a newly elected representative to the Tripartite Confederacy she was finding this difficult. Currently her life seemed to be a battle between herself and the malevolent forces of post-post-modern technology. It could hardly even be called technology anymore; it seemed to have developed an evil will of its own, though it was dangerous to say such a thing or even to think it.

"My spies are everywhere," came an unattributed quote floating through her head. At one time she would have assumed this was a memory, but that was no longer assured. She had been delighted with the upgrade that allowed her to speak, read, and understand Farsi, Somali, Spanish, and Arabic within minutes of transmission, as well as shoring up her somewhat rusty German. She was a linguist and a writer—a multilingual grammar nerd. At first, the required five minutes of advertising that came every two hours had seemed like a small price to pay.

And right on cue, here they came! She ducked instinctively, as one attacked by a swarm of mosquitos, though this was ridiculous, because they were *inside* her head.

Woopie Cola, *It's* So *Great!*
Buy some now and *don't be late*!
Take it on your *VIR*-tual date!
Woopie Cola *seals* your *fate!*

She hated the way "virtual" didn't really fit and had to be chanted speedily. (At least she wasn't required to sing along, though there was a proposal before the Board.) Now it was playing again. And again. On an apparently endless loop.

Oh, hell, alright, thought Olivia, blinking twice to purchase two gallons of the horrible stuff. It tasted like carbonated prunes fried in manure. It didn't matter, she could pour it out as long as she remembered to first adjust the mirrored door that reflected the sink.

Anyway, the ability to buy the stuff easily and quickly was a godsend; it meant she'd have no more ads for a precious two hours and might actually be able to get something done.

Olivia's ultimate designator, what used to be hilariously called a "last name,"[2] was Squidlight because she was a descendent of the Originators—those who, in the misty legends of prehistory, were supposed to have begun the framework which now interpreted sentient life on all known planes and dimensions of being. She wondered if one of them in their wisdom had anticipated the problem of commercials going off in your head all the time. If not, how had they failed to anticipate something so obvious? If so, why had they not addressed the issue?

Something stirred vaguely in her memory, something from one of the many Sage Chronicles whose transcripts it was one of her jobs to study ... *but which's? If you can say "whose," shouldn't you be able to say "which's"?* It can be seen by the sudden intrusion of this thought that she probably carried some of the genes and mental processing of Sophie McGregor, and perhaps also of the legendary Halycon Sage himself.

Olivia briefly considered the Ancestors, sometimes known as The Twelve, though she had always thought this sounded pretentious. Halycon Sage, TechieSquid, Nano Prime One, Ruby Echevaria, Fatty Lumpkin, No-Name Stupid, Augustus Rathbone, Deandra Hollandaise, Nuri ibn-Abdurraheem, Sophie McGregor, a Snrrr and ... who was the other one? She could never remember the

---

2 In case you're wondering what's wrong with "last name"—and we make a quick SquidSign of protection as we explain this—if any being laid claim to a last name, it would obviously be the immediate end of that being and all other embodied physical beings, requiring the whole miserable business of individualized manifestation to be done all over again.

other one. They represented beings of different types, just as the ever-ruling Circles of Twelve must represent each of The Great Races (also supposed to be the name of an ancient "movie.") Twelve of them in all, a mystic number from way back.

It was rumored that at one time near the dawn of history different types of beings did not mix their DNA either physically or artificially. Robots were robots, not even thought to be sentient. Animals were animals, people were people, and space aliens and interdimensional arrivals were also thought to remain strictly within their own lines of development. This seemed improbable. It was *also* rumored that at one time there was only one of everybody. Olivia sighed. Life must have been so uncomplicated back then. Sometimes she quietly yearned for those simple, primitive days.

She reined in her thoughts. (*Rained? Reigned?*) This wasn't getting any work done. But it *was* one of her subsidiary duties to study the works of Sage and his—*what's* the opposite of a progenitor? Oh, honestly! And his literary descendants, the creators of the Post-Modernist Minimalist Neo-Symbolist Pseudo-Realist School of Literature.

So perhaps it was alright if she suspended her other occupations to hunt down the quotation. Something Sage himself had said.[3]

Though the ultimate designator Squidlight was also associated with the religion, Olivia, though of course she respected it, stayed well away. It was just not her thing. [NOTE: Humans seem overrepresented in the Circle of Twelve schematic. It is possible that Ms. Squidlight is missing some aliens, or even possibly some other humans. This configuration of twelve is not definitive.]

Alexander Preisczech—if it *was* Alexander Preisczech—was working on his new formula, which not only had the elegance required of true mathematics but looked like solving some of the most intractable problems of the new society. He admired it, sitting so pristine on his blackboard (which was green, but he could never bring himself to call it a greenboard, though the recurring thought of this linguistic and practical conflict bothered him every time he looked at it.) But for now, he could merely enjoy his formula, conscious of a job well done, before moving from theoretical to applied science. There it was in all its simple beauty.

---

3 "Sage knew that the television was even worse for him than the junk food. It was soothing on a superficial level, but it sapped his strength and robbed his dreams of meaning. His mind was becoming a scratchy recording device that played back mediocre hit songs he didn't even like, news of bombings and shootings, the faces of annoying celebrities. *As a man thinketh, so is he.*" – The Way Beyond

SU^{x}2$_b$U or maybe SuX^{2}BU

[NOTE: We at the Squid & Sage Editorial Board are writers, critics, and literary or sociological scholars, not hard scientists or mathematicians. If we have rendered this formula incorrectly, we are sorry. However, it is pronounced as spelled, and its effect when applied in the real world is as described within these pages.]

CHAPTER TWO

FAR FUTURE AGAIN

lady who may or may not have been Olivia Squidlight of the year 1.1.1212, or author Deandra Hollendaise or somebody else glided quietly down the breezeway outside the Center for All Religions Temple and House of Governance, a much more magnificent edifice even than its name suggests.

The ancestry of this lady was mixed: human, Squid, and possibly more. You couldn't really tell to look at her, except that there was something flowing in the way she moved, an elegant grace. She was tall and thin, and sometimes her deep blue eyes took on improbable shades of purple, or green, or even magenta. Was she the original or one of the knock-offs? But who really knew anymore, and, after all, did it matter? It was better not to ask.

Within the lovely, big temple complex—which combined the best of the architect Sinan's Ottoman mosques, the labyrinthine gardens of earlier and later times, and all from the plant and animal worlds that was most lushly beautiful—a meeting of the Joint Religious and Ruling Council was going on. Already, the participants were not happy campers. The meeting was called to order and a request was made for all participants to state their names. The twelve designated spots around the table were all filled, and seating (floating, beaming-in, whatever) for others was provided in concentric circles around the central area.

The Chair[4] opens the meeting:
Board members, please respond as I call your names. Icky Bicky Ittle Wiggly?
Here.
Deandra Hollendaise?
I'm *obviously* present. See my new dress?
Halycon Sage?
Here.
Halycon Sage?
Here.
Alexander Preisczech?
Here.
TechieSquid?

---

4 Why anyone would be referred to as a "chair"—an inanimate and nonspeaking piece of "furniture" still sometimes used by bipedal beings with bending knees—is incomprehensible, but tradition must be honored, especially in these time-hallowed institutions.

Here.
Halycon Sage?
Here.
Halycon Sage?
Here.

Suddenly the barely begun meeting was disrupted. Halycon Sage stood in the doorway, watching this madness in disbelief. Yes, there were four of him other than himself, all identical, and all had answered in his very own voice.

Startled out of both embarrassment and good manners, he broke with precedent and also broke a strong taboo hitherto shared by himself, imaginary author Karima Vargas Bushnell, and writer/researcher Sophie McGregor

As you who have read The Sage Chronicles will surely recall, Sage and the other characters around him never swear. They use coy little asterisks[5] and substitutions.

While there was an occasional hell or damn, and one instance of a slightly ruder word in connection with literary critic Basel Vasselschnauzer, there was little or no serious swearing. All three of the aforementioned real or imaginary characters felt that, while swearing was shocking and fun in the 1970s, by the 1990s or so, it had become a bore.

---

5 This word is not *asterix*! (Nor is there any such word as nuculer; it's *nuclear*.)

Halycon Sage looked at the raised platform and the twelve participants, four of whom were indisputably himself.

"What the *actual fuck?*" asked Halycon Sage in a loud, penetrating voice. Quickly, the meeting was adjourned.

CHAPTER THREE

THE IN-BETWEEN SPACE

Sage was not very comfortable in the Flexible In-Between Space, though of course its look, feel, sound, and smell were perfectly aligned with his unconscious expectations. This meant it looked, felt, sounded, and smelled like Dry Creek Gulch. The rain-on-sage-and-dust smell coming up from the ground was there, what he had learned to call petracore, as was the winding away of the Truckee River, banked by willow and poplar trees, and the purple, snow-topped mountains in the background. It was the ordinary view he saw from the window of his little writing room every day, and he was sitting in his ordinary writing chair.

This perfect effect was rather spoiled, though, by what he saw when he swiveled around and confronted the *rest* of the room, placing his back toward the comforting and familiar view. He was on the stage of his old theatre department at the University of Nevada, Reno. Though his memory remained spotty, like a foggy landscape broken up by patches of sun, he had recovered this fragment along with the fact that he had been too shy to act, but had enjoyed painting sets during rehearsal periods and working the lighting board on show nights.

Still, he was not altogether pleased with the weird combination of things he remembered from different times and places. In front of him, where the audience should have been, were platforms of different shapes and sizes, each occupied by some type of living being.

A few Squids, check. He remembered the Squidren well. (Even aside from his lingering amnesia, it was a chancy matter what information would accompany the traveler to one of these meetings.) A Nanobot, looking inordinately pleased with itself. No surprise there. Sophie McGregor, Basel Vasselschnauzer, a few more of the old gang from the village. (Sage had taken endless guff from the townspeople for calling Dry Creek Gulch a village, something caused by his multicultural upbringing. But now he did it on purpose. Because he knew it was annoying.)

His eyes travelled around the circle of beings, resting at last on the undoubted reason he was here: the four identical Halycon Sages sitting innocently side by side, waiting for the meeting to begin. The scene faded and a new scene appeared.

Ah, yes, the psychiatrist's office. Sage recognized that as well. Though he had never been crazy or even particularly troubled, he had drawn the attention of this profession at one point in his life by incautiously mentioning some of his visions, revealing the fact of his almost nonexistent memory, and even more recklessly admitting in a moment of misplaced confidence, that he had rather enjoyed some of the more sparkly entertainments of the 1970s. Of course, all of this was reported to the authorities, and predictably a course of talk therapy was prescribed. He had also unwisely admitted that he sometimes drank beer, causing a deep inquiry into possible alcoholism.

Though Sage appeared to be Native American and was certainly partly so, he apparently had enough mixed blood to have dodged this particular bullet. Or maybe he was just lucky. As he spoke with the fortunately friendly and sympathetic therapist, it was discovered that his little psychedelic adventures had done him no harm, that his visions were previous and unconnected, and that they were not only a positive force in his life, but also quite in compliance with the traditions of his probable ancestors.

It had been determined that Sage had none of the markers that would have fitted him for the psychiatrist's couch; he downplayed the amnesia and having become rather good at this, was able to conceal it. Yet apparently that particular couch and chair arrangement stood for comfort and confidence in his mind, so they had appeared here where it was necessary for him to receive some possibly disturbing information.

CHAPTER FOUR

PREISCZECH EXPLAINS

"**M**y friend, I can explain to you the whole thing, and it isn't so bad really. Actually, I'm surprised you haven't shown up here before now."

Sage looked at Alexander Preisczech in equal surprise. The last time Sage had seen him, the inventor was tweaking a new formula designed to fix a specific problem he said would appear in the far future. How he knew *that* was anybody's guess, as was the reason he had turned up here in the Indeterminate In-Between Space, apparently ready to shed light and answer questions.

"Shoot," said Sage.

"Well, I don't know how much you remember …" Preisczech sounded slightly apologetic. He always found the issue of Sage's spotty memory potentially embarrassing, though Sage himself had no problem discussing it.

"What do you know about the current status of Dry Creek Gulch?"

"We can't get out," said Sage. "At least only into the mountains or along the river for ceremonies and hunting and stuff. The wall seals itself behind us and opens when we return, and it won't let in anybody new." He stopped with satisfaction. *Nothing wrong with my memory now,* he thought.

"Well, do you remember that the Squidren absolutely deny being the ones now keeping us in? They certainly admit to imposing the *original* wall, but they insist they abandoned it after the nuclear explosion and the do-over."

Hmm, this was a bit vaguer in the author's mind. He wasn't really sure if he remembered.

"Uh-huh," he said, playing along. "I know we mostly can't get out anymore."

"But *you* are out," replied the other. Yes, that was true.

"Do you remember this room?"

"Well, it's a combination of two different rooms that have nothing to do with each other, so I must conclude that it's an illusion. But quite a comfortable one, though a little temporally muddled."

Though he kept this to himself, Sage was an expert on temporal muddle. After all this time, he still didn't know if he had been a young man in the 1970s or had heard all those stories of the hippie days from some older person, a gifted storyteller apparently. Because of this, and because he was not aging very fast, he had no idea how old he really was. "Someplace between 30 and 50," he told inquirers facetiously, but he really couldn't get much nearer than that.

"Do you know how you got here?" asked Preisczech.

"I just kind of turned up," said Sage.

"You had an appointment."

Sage remained silent. If his old friend wanted to tell him something, he would. Suddenly Sage was assailed by doubt. Was this really Preisczech? He retained a trace of his accent, which all the village ladies had thought so charming, but his word order was mostly straightened out. Could this have happened in a mere six months? Or maybe it was years. The doubt came back, stronger than ever, a sudden doubting of everyone and everything.

"Do you understand why there are five of you now?"

Suddenly the weird experience in the temple came back to him.

"Oh, that," he said rather flatly.

"Yes, that." Preisczech brightened up, nodding in satisfaction. "Don't worry, my friend. I explain to you so clear you never forget. I explain to you *everything*."

Apparently Preisczech's English still went a little off kilter when he got excited. Sage was glad. He would have missed it.

Preisczech swung his leather swivel chair around from his computer(ish) and fixed Sage with an intense gaze.

"Now pay attention, I'll try to make this as simple as possible. There used to be just one of everybody. Make sense so far?"

Sage nodded. Though still affected by periodic cloud banks of amnesia and confusion due to constant micro-shifts between perspectives and dimensions—and thank *Wakan Tanka* he at least understood what was happening now—Sage was pretty sure that he grasped this basic concept, that there was just one of everybody, no more and no less.

"No *fewer!*" shouted a passing Mad Grammarian, whose telepathic abilities appeared somewhat beyond the ordinary. Sage abruptly corrected himself mentally and added a lightning-fast Squidish-style apology thought for any offense given. He returned from this micro-interaction to find Preisczech staring at him with barely controlled intensity. He was aware of how Sage was sometimes caught by random drifting realities and had learned that patience was better than arguing.

"But *not any more!*" he continued. "Now there are at least five or six of almost everybody, even not counting the *time-ghost-fan selves*, which increase the numbers into the millions. But never mind that for now," he told the startled Sage. "I give you brochure. I have many brochure." In a sure sign that he was growing excited again, or maybe impatient, Preisczech's English was going increasingly wonky. "Here, I demonstrate on fingers the ways that post-individual selves are created. Not necessarily in order of frequency or historical appearance or any other criteria, just as I think of them."

CHAPTER FIVE

IN DRY CREEK GULCH

Dateline: The Amorphous Present
of the Previous Novels

I wonder why she called us together, thought Emma, drawing the gauze curtain aside and looking out the big bay window. Brilliant sunlight streamed in as four of the more prominent citizens of Dry Creek Gulch approached the ~~Dirty Dog Bar~~ Canis Fidelis Cafe and Juice Bar.[6] Seeing them together was unusual.

First came Sophie McGregor, former high school valedictorian, upcoming literary light, and invaluable member of the Green Thread Team that handled organic farming and water management for the town. Well, the Blue Thread Team was also involved with Water, of course. By unspoken but universal consent, the town had

---

6 Okay, we really have to stop this crossing-out nonsense for the bar/cafe! It will annoy readers past the breaking point. What are we going to call the place? Make up your damn minds! — the Editors

adopted the Squidren's names for the different spheres of community activity. They liked the color designations, and threads sounded less pompous than committees.

The second person approaching was Deandra Hollendaise, sometime romance writer, gossip, minor troublemaker and second-rate imitator of Halycon Sage. She was the founder, as she proudly declared to all, of the Heaving Bodice Romance Division of the Post-Modernist Minimalist Neo-Symbolist Pseudo-Realist School of Literature.

Ordinarily Sophie avoided Hollendaise like the plague, and she had once prevailed upon Sage to take her out of his literary cannon altogether, or at least to exclude her from the Three Major Works associated with *The Book of Squidly Light*. (Sage had later withdrawn his consent, feeling it unfair to wipe someone out of existence merely because they were annoying.) Sophie had no use for Deandra, yet here they were together, high heels clicking in unison up the wooden ramp to the Dirty Dog, as though they were the best of friends. Or no, that was wrong. Sophie was not a heels kind of person and was wearing clogs. The second heel-clicker was Squidress Four. She was doing that shape-shifting thing some Squidresses did, appearing part human and part alien, the two shapes melting back and forth in a kind of dance.

So far Emma had never seen the male or Zi Squidren do this. It was a female thing only, and should have looked appalling, but was actually quite beautiful and graceful in a strange way. And, as usual, *some* onlookers saw only the human while others saw only the Squid. Emma could always see both, and so could Sophie.

The fourth person approaching with them was Jenny.

Emma showed the little party to a comfortable red leather booth[7] and poured their coffee, steaming hot and delicious. Moving with her usual swift grace, she took their orders back to Preisczech, then returned and slid into the booth beside them.

Preisczech was cooking today. Everyone in town was showing unexpected talents and his OCD, or whatever it was, had made him a careful and precise cook. Besides the normal western cooking and other stuff he'd picked up from Jenny, he'd reportedly learned some amazing dishes from a grandmother back in the Czech Republic.

By purposely walking ahead of Deandra, Sophie was hoping to exclude her annoying presence from the table, which was designed for four people only. No such luck. With a dazzling smile, Deandra squeezed in. *Rats*, thought Sophie.

Squidress Four called the meeting to order. While Jenny the Squid Empress outranked her by orders of magnitude, she usually preferred remaining in the background and in human form: the second-best cook in Dry Creek Gulch and affectionate wife to Alexander Preisczech. (As nihilist writer Neimand Kompt had once remarked, the lovey-doviness of this couple was fit to make anyone sick.)

---

7 No, of course not real leather. Think Perkins or Denny's in the 1970s.

"So, what's going on, Ms. Four?" asked Emma. "Why are we here?"

"It's this literary conference," replied Four, momentarily wishing she could actually *eat* the pancakes. It was strange to be wanting something more substantial than the Squid's usual diet of light. But the smell was delicious anyway, so there was that to enjoy.

"There seems to be an inflection point in the next few weeks, and there's a danger of misdirection."

Four had been consulting with TechieSquid, who was still nerding it up on the SquidShip, rarely setting tentacle on land, but having a wonderful time. She'd also spoken with several other shape-shifters and time travellers and had some idea of the event that was approaching for good or ill. She was downplaying the situation, not wanting to cause a panic. Somehow it was connected with the conference, though she wasn't yet sure how.

Gathering her concentration, Squidress Four telepathically shared a brief scene from one of Sage's books, one he hadn't yet written.[8] You'll find this scene again in its proper context, when it actually happens, beginning on p. 60 of this manuscript. Because that's where Squidress Four got it, just a little way into the future. Though the scene appeared before them like a movie, she was also reading it like a book and had

---

8 Unknown speaker: Wait, what? I thought Karima Vargas Bushnell was writing these books. And now you're saying it's Sage? An Editor: *No!* We're not going to go there, do you understand? Who made up who and all of that. Just no!

donned an outrageous pair of purple cat-eye glasses to enhance the effect. She condensed it a little so as not to irritate her listeners.

"As Sage stood contemplating on the sidewalk," she read, "a thin young man with brown hair, a clean-shaven face, and no personality whatsoever appeared suddenly and handed him a sheaf of papers.

"'What's this?' asked Halycon Sage, looking remarkably blank.

"'These are the newest mini-novels we have,' said the young man reverently. 'From your Post-Modernist Minimalist Neo-Symbolist Pseudo-Realist School of Literature that you founded. The School has developed quite a lot since you last checked in with us. Here's a good one,' he added. 'I *like* this one.'

"He offered another paper. Sage took it gingerly while a few passersby craned their necks over to have a look. Here is what he read.

<u>Baraboo Bartholomew, Fur Trapper with a Heart</u>
by Wade Garnette

Baraboo Bartholomew was a hungry guy, and if you look at the title of this novel, you can see why.

The End

"'What?' asked Halycon Sage, looking blanker still. A moment later he laughed. 'Okay, that was not too bad.'"

Abruptly the scene conjured up by Squidress Four dissolved, disturbed by the sudden appearance of Ruby, which had broken her concentration. Instead of walking into the cafe in the normal manner, Ruby had appeared out of nowhere next to the table, accompanied by a noise like an exploding firecracker. She looked a bit dusty like someone returning from a long journey, which in fact she was. Nobody, not even Halycon Sage, had seen her in weeks.

Various humans and Squidren exclaimed in surprise.

"Budge over," said Ruby, squeezing into the booth, which now apparently held six.

"I'll explain later. Right now, we have a possible neo-apocalyptic event shaping up for this time and place, and we need all our resources to deal with it."

She and Four exchanged a look and Four nodded. They were definitely on the same page.

"And the only thing *that can really mess things up,* taking everybody's time and attention," continued Ruby, "is this *STUPID* Literary Conference!

"It doesn't seem like much, but remember that poem about the horseshoe nail? Little things can snowball and spiral into big things."

There was another loud bang as No-Name Stupid shoved open the wooden cover over the only window in the Dirty Dog Bar / Canis Fidelis Cafe and Gathering Place that had no glass. It had been specially altered to accommodate him, for Stupid was a horse.

He was mostly indifferent to the incomprehensible human concerns of the Committees, but he had heard his own name spoken, was a poet himself, and was further attracted by the mention of a *horseshoe nail*, a subject of obvious relevance to his sphere of influence. He thought he might add something of importance.[9]

---

9 In case you don't remember and don't have *The Book of Squidly Light* handy to check this reference, "For want of a nail, the shoe was lost, for want of a shoe, the horse was lost, for want of a horse, the rider was lost, for want of a rider the battle was lost, for want of a battle the kingdom was lost, all for the want of a horseshoe nail."

CHAPTER SIX

PREISCZECH CONTINUES

Just as he had promised, Preisczech was still—or again, or whatever, as time in the In-Between Space was problematic—enumerating on his fingers the various ways that what had been a single being could quickly or slowly split into many.

1. **<u>Time Travel</u>**. If someone lives a long life but also at some point travels into the future, this creates *two* of them: the one whose life moves through time in the ordinary way, and the one who has traveled. They do not merge into a single entity. While not all details are correct, the now-difficult-to-find short story *We're Coming Through the Window* explains this phenomenon with fair accuracy.

2. **<u>Uploading</u>**. If someone's consciousness including all their memories, characteristics, and mannerisms—the whole enchilada—is uploaded into the Netverse, that

consciousness can be downloaded into a new body at any time, even while the original person continues to exist.

3. **Theft**. Around 2024, give or take, the ancients came up with something called Generative AI. This technology was stealing actors' and singers' voices, writers' writing, painters' paintings, and copying their styles, stealing any kind of creative content to copy it, and often you couldn't tell the real stuff from the copies.

Sage opened his mouth to speak, but Preisczech held up his hand like a white-gloved policeman in a cartoon.

"Wait, I know you don't see the connection yet. Just gimme a sec."

Ah, his slang has gotten better, thought Sage.

"So, at some point after you died, somebody started writing new Halycon Sage novels, flooding the market with them."

"I know about the imitators," said Sage. "After all, the Post-Modernist Minimalist Neo-Symbolist Pseudo-Realist School of Literature couldn't be just one person."

"No, no, I'm not talking about that. People were stealing your ideas and style to the point where nobody could tell the difference, and this might not've been a big deal in Post-Event Dry Creek Gulch, but in the Alternate Universe, where you were still a household word, it was a *very* big deal."

Sage sighed. "Well, that's kind of a bummer, but if I've been dead for a thousand years or so, it doesn't really matter. Not a major deal."

"You still don't understand," said Preisczech. This technology evolved. At a certain point, they couldn't just copy people's styles, mannerisms, voices, physical forms, and creative content. They could copy *whole people*."

Oh. Sage was beginning to see why there might be so many of him running around, metaphorically bumping into each other.

4. **Cryogenics**. Same deal. If someone is frozen before less cumbersome methods of life preservation are invented, reawakens and is dumped into a new body because the original is poorly preserved, but the authorities rule that the original should still be allowed to exist, this *also* creates an alternate self.

This is getting awfully complicated, thought Sage.

Preisczech paused to add a random thought.

"Of course, if all these new bodies had not been identical to the originals, a great deal of confusion could have been avoided. But, unfortunately and understandably, those synthesizing the new bodies out of rejuvenated corpse parts, animal parts, lab grown cells, or by any other method took great care to make the new body identical to the old one in every detail. They succeeded to the point where there was no way of telling which of these identicals was the true or original individual. As you can imagine, this caused enormous confusion in relation to property, marriage, and every other aspect of life."

He paused a moment in thought. "Made the lawyers happy, though."

Sage was about to interrupt but was faced with the policeman hand again.

"There are a few more," said his friend calmly.

5. **Fanning**. (In the intensity of his communication, Preisczech had forgotten he'd intended to use a brochure for this one.)

"Every thought creates a new reality. Have you ever been driving down the street and you suddenly see yourself in a car crash? Only takes a second, but vivid, vivid! Or maybe you suddenly imagine yourself in front of a phalanx of cameras and an ecstatic audience as you accept some sort of scientific prize."

Sage nodded. His related experiences centered around horses and literature, but yeah, the sensation was familiar.

"Each of these episodes creates a self. Probable and possible selves spread outward like a fan; even the most momentary and idle thoughts of doing something or going somewhere generate a new time-ghost self.

"Oh, and there's one more. You should know about the SwitchingUp technology as well. *That* added another level of complication."

"Switching up? What's that?" asked Sage.

"My friend, the hour grows late, and I am tired with all this explaining. And I'm due in Somalia in five minutes. Here, read this." He handed Sage a booklet. *SWITCHING UP*™, the title read. Sage opened to the first page.

CHAPTER SEVEN

THE HISTORY OF SWITCHING UP™

Preisczech was abruptly gone. Sage was getting a bit tired of the Amorphous In-Between Space. Right now it was showing the familiar view of Dry Creek Gulch through a suddenly appearing window: a pale brown expanse of land accompanied by blue sky, fleecy white clouds, purple snow-capped mountains, the little winding river bordered by willow trees—the whole nine yards. He wished he were back there, but was pretty sure this was only part of the illusion designed to make him comfortable. At the moment it appeared to be the only game in town.

The only game in town, he thought. He was getting so tired of these stupid sports and gambling analogies. The latter might be a peculiarity of Nevada in particular. If you grew up there in the 1960s, you couldn't avoid them. They were stuck in your head even if you had no interest in either sports or gambling. And either Sage or somebody whose memories he shared had definitely grown up there during that time period. Maybe someday he would know which.

Stupid amnesia! Stupid everything! He was tired and bored and ready to go home to No-Name Stupid, who was the least stupid person he knew.

But since the only way out of this seemed to be through it, he bent over page 1 of SwitchingUp™. This is what he read.

When the SwitchingUp™ technology was first released, it was a great shock to everyone. Initially considered just another pointless tweak for cluttering up the post-post-modern mind, it allowed anyone using it to feel exactly what another person was feeling for one minute and 37 seconds. You wouldn't think this would be such a big deal, but actually it changed everything.

There were many surprises.

"*That's* what you've been complaining about all this time? You've got to be kidding me!" Or, "You've been living with *that* for 25 years? How could you even get up in the morning?"

Compassion increased as those who had never known depression or hell-states got a quick but powerful introduction. "There were depths below as black and hollow as a starless night, and people lived there, married there and had children, paid their rent and taxes, walked in the free air and nobody hauled them off to shock treatments or manacles."[10]

The new technology made compassion and empathy real. These qualities had been trained out of many people by the stupid thoughtlessness of the age. "Go kill yourself, because nobody cares," was a common comment on social media. The people making such comments weren't evil, as might have been suspected before life was lived online. They merely lacked imagination, and their minds had never been trained, or only enough to bat insults back and forth like ping pong balls, imagining themselves to have won something.

It worked the other way too. Those who had never known boundless, overflowing joy now stood under its blissful waterfall. People lay on the grass laughing, listening to birds. For those who had not known love, the same. The tidal wave of passion that connected hearts, minds, and bodies, or the sweetness of a charmed and protective love for a child or an animal.

Those who'd never known responsibility tasted it now: the crushing or grounding or inspiring weight of dedication to a cherished ideal, someone dear, or something it was one's duty to

---

10 Damon Knight, "Be My Guest," in *The Others*, Terry Carr Ed. Story first published in 1958.

protect. Hope and inspiration were tasted as well, a revelation to all who'd formerly sleepwalked through their lives on auto-pilot.

Though the intervention ended in less than two minutes, even one of these encounters changed a person forever, and it could happen anywhere at any moment. (Due to a variety of factors, the originally subscriber-based technology quickly burst its banks and flooded into the general population. Before long no purchase or thoughtful decision was necessary.)

One of the greatest consequences, unforeseen by those who thought idealism, philosophy, and religion were nonsense, was that the technology bridged the chasm between those who thought life was meaningful and those who did not.

Within the 21st Century science of Neurotheology,[11] which explored ecstatic mystical states through the lens of the brain, research subjects across a spectrum of religions, nature practices, and logical frameworks reported five elements: connectedness, clarity, intensity, surrender, and transformation. These experiences of hyper-reality and ultimate interconnection were self-confirming, bringing unshakable conviction of their validity to the experiencers, if not to the baffled friends and relatives.

---

11 Andrew B. Newberg, *Principles of Neurotheology.*

Before SwitchingUp™, those who hadn't had the experience could dismiss these encounters as wishful thinking, imagination, a brain chemical high, or some variation of, "Wow, that's a really cool sunset!" As with all individual perceptions, there was no way to share it convincingly with the skeptical.

Now they could. For one minute and 37 seconds, anyone who happened to run into the right person could experience the self-affirming essentiality, goodness, and mind-blowing hyper-reality of the Multiverse. And this turned out to be a real game-changer.

Through the evolution of technology over decades and centuries, humanity was either becoming less human, or expanding its capacity. You could look at it either way. Each new development took something away, but added something else. Author Karima Vargas Bushnell once knew a person who wouldn't send emails to her recently found intellectual companions and soulmates because she thought that form of communication was inauthentic, not like really being with someone. Yet this medium allowed people to be instantly in touch with those on the other side of the world. This objection seemed quaint and unnecessary to the imaginary author.

Surely when the telephone was invented, there were people who thought the absence of the physical person—being in their presence, seeing their face, sensing their aura of thoughts and scents and what have you—was an unholy violation of the relationship. Yet how sweet and intimate to hold the phone close to your ear and hear the clear tones of the beloved friend so far away.

Complaints had been made that television trafficked in a form of graven images. These were dismissed as the ravings of luddites or religious fanatics. How far was too far, and when did the human-machine hybrids cease to be in any sense human? That was the question.

Just as Sage finished reading the first page of the pamphlet, there was a knock on the door and Preisczech was back. Their conversation continued as though there had been no break.

"So, are these other versions of me *ghost images* like what you described as ..." Sage thought for a moment. "Fan selves?"

"Oh no, they're fully realized. They might not agree with you all the time, though. Or with each other," Preisczech added. "Any change in anything creates variations, regardless of whether things test out as being identical. You never get an exact copy of anything once experience and personal choice kick in. Even in molecules."

Molecules have personal choice? thought Sage, but it was too late to ask. The scene blinked out and he was somewhere else.

CHAPTER EIGHT

DRY CREEK GULCH AGAIN

Dateline: The Amorphous Present of the Previous Novels

The scene was the twice-monthly Team Meeting at the ~~Dirty Dog Bar~~ Canis Fidelis Bar and Grill a couple of weeks after we last visited. Besides the Committee Heads,[12] a number of other interested citizens were there, as well as some rubbernecks who just had nothing better to do or had come in for pancakes. There was quite a crowd. It was good that the juice bar and grill had apparently expanded a bit.

Life was proceeding normally in Dry Creek Gulch, if such an adjective could possibly apply to the ridiculous,

---

12 Sage always pictured a bunch of disembodied heads sitting around on the cafe table. Bloody or not, the image was pretty unpleasant. Yuck!

post-apocalyptic situation. (*Adverb*, commented Sage's inner editor. "*Normally*" *is an adverb, not an adjective. Modifies the verb, ends in LY.*)

"*No duh,*" said Sophie, sounding more than usually like a teenager. *Huh?* thought Sage. This was odd. Either he had mumbled his grammatical correction unawares or Sophie had become psychic. So unstrung from the anchor of normal reality had everything become that either was quite possible.[13]

Shut up, snarled the other half of Sage's brain, the creative half, to his inner editor. *I'm writing here. Shut up till I'm ready for you.*

With all the interventions of the Squidren and other aliens, including sea creatures and sentient fungus, it should have been impossible to do *anything*.

As we were trying to say when we were so rudely interrupted, life was proceeding as normal, almost uncannily so. The scientific brigade among the villagers had figured out the practical matters of food, water, heat, lighting, and so on with amazing perspicuity. (That's perspicacity combined with acuity.)

The apparent normality of life was strange, because between the Nanobots taking apart every machine and technology on earth with minor exceptions and the *other* drastic changes caused by both the Nanobots and the Squidren, including the collapse of the entire underlying

---

13 "Backward run sentences till reels the mind," once read a humorous description of *Time Magazine's* writing style from some forgotten wit.

structure of modern and post-modern civilization, *nothing* should have been normal.

The key ingredient, of course, was Halycon Sage's imagination. If he thought something should work, it would, whether or not it made any sense. And if he chose to ignore some scientific truth, focusing instead on plot, character development, and the things that really interested him, that problem simply went away.

This made reality unstable, though, because the oddly patched parts of it were held together only by Sage's belief or complete non-attention. Preisczech and the other scientists in the village were concerned that if Sage ever really noticed what was going on, everything would fall apart.[14] They worked hard to take protective measures, like assiduously keeping him away from Sophie's scientific library lectures on How Things Work.

Though not as strong as Sage's, the thoughts and opinions of others in town apparently had some influence as well. Aside from things Sage was interested in, the normality of the village apparently reflected a consensus of whatever the townspeople *considered* to be normal.

---

14 See the short story *It's a Good Life* by Jerome Bixby.

CHAPTER NINE

CONCERNING THE LITERARY CONFERENCE

As we read just a few moments ago in Chapter Eight, normality in the village apart from Sage's influence apparently consisted of whatever the *townspeople* considered to be normal.

While the park, library, and playground remained, as well as a nice cafe—the well-known and beloved Dirty Dog Bar, now transformed into the Canis Fidelis Grill and Juice Bar or whatever people were calling it that day—a quaint little downtown shopping district had grown up around them, spreading up and down the street in either direction.

There was no mall, as apparently the dislike that one or more citizens held for them was stronger than the bland, unthinking desire of others for their own convenience. The worried scientists in town, including

Sophie, Preisczech, and former airline pilot and current inventor Mohammed Abdurraheem Hussein, were pretty sure that the mental and emotional energy—let's call it the candle power or wattage—of each person in town affected the consensus reality in proportion to its intensity. There was even a theory that some *animals* were affecting reality, but most had not bought into this idea yet; they had enough trouble without this additional complicating factor.

While the place still *looked* like Dry Creek Gulch, the main street was full of quaint little shops and postmodern tech startups. Would any of the tech in these places actually *work?* That was apparently up to Preisczech, either because he'd found a way of controlling the tech-dismantling Nanobots after the loss of the deceptively cheap-looking tin whistle that had formerly ruled them, or because he was the only major character or prominent citizen who actually gave a damn.

The managers and employees of these establishments, being at the moment mere lay figures not even bearing names, were not able to influence reality. But you never could tell what might emerge in the future. Look at the cat Fatty Lumpkin, who started out as an unnamed orange cat in a two-sentence reference and subsequently became so important that several other characters filed a petition complaining about his undue prominence.[15]

A few doors down from the Dirty Dog, a sign announced the opening of a new law firm, though what

---

15 See Part Five: Fatty Lumpkin, Esq. in *Sage's Multiverse Mini-Series.*

exactly it would do in Dry Creek Gulch was quite a puzzle. There was also a rumor that Edwin Puppy, Esq., about whom nobody knew very much, was preparing to join the firm.

Spreading toward the outskirts of town to the north and south (and suddenly unpaved one day because people apparently preferred it that way), Main Street now included a candy store, a shoe and saddle repair shop that dealt in leather work, the House of Cats, and Crazy Melvin's Monster Radio Store. There was also a big sign, emblazoned with a blue whale or leaping dolphin or some such thing, which read,

Cetacean Nation: Come See What We're Up To!

("Up to about a thousand pounds," joked a passer-by.)

Next to the sign was a little booth displaying intricate clothing and jewelry designs, reading *Cetacean Creations*. The empty chair, presumably to be occupied by the proprietor of this small establishment, was oddly shaped. Very oddly.

The oddness did not bother Sage; oddness never did. The disappearance of commercialism had been the one clear benefit he'd found in the End of the World, and some days he thought it was almost worth it. But now it seemed to be creeping back.

He momentarily considered just getting rid of the new little shopping district. While it appeared to be trying hard, it wasn't real yet, and if he put his mind to it, it never would be.

As he stood contemplating on the sidewalk, a thin young man with brown hair, a clean-shaven face, and no personality whatsoever, handed him some papers. Sage suspected he was one of the new amorphous characters who were hanging around lately, possibly trying to become real.

"What's this?" asked Halycon Sage, looking remarkably blank.

"Well, these are the newest mini-novels," said the man. He was suddenly wearing horn-rimmed glasses. "From your Post-Modernist Minimalist Neo-Symbolist Pseudo-Realist School of Literature. The School has developed quite a lot since you last checked in with us," he added with a vague show of enthusiasm.

He had apparently decided to become a publisher or bookseller, giving increased solidity and definition to his form and personality.

"What's your name?" asked Sage conversationally. "I assume you *have* one."

"Err," said the man, like Sage, looking remarkably blank. It seemed he wasn't prepared for this question.

"Never mind," said Sage kindly. "You'll get there if you're supposed to." He thought for a moment to see if he could name the guy. No, he had nothing.

"*Here's* a good one," said the brown-haired man, abruptly changing the subject. "I *like* this one."

He offered a piece of paper. Sage took it gingerly, while a few other shadowy figures craned their necks over to see what was going on. Here is what he read.

<u>Baraboo Bartholomew, Fur Trapper with a Heart</u>
by Wade Garnette

Baraboo Bartholomew was a hungry guy, and if you look at the title of this novel, you can see why.

The End

"What?" said Halycon Sage. A moment later he laughed. "Okay, that was not too bad."

CHAPTER TEN

CONCERNING DEANDRA

Now came Deandra Hollendaise, about the last person he wanted to see, clicking up to him on blue suede heels about four inches high. Watching her navigate the cracked sidewalks and dusty intervals in those things aroused an unwilling admiration in Sage. He had to give the woman credit, she really was good at some things. And she looked rather nice too. (Ruby had been away for a long time, and Sage had no earthly or unearthly idea where she was.)

Hollendaise put her hand on the characterless young man's elbow and looked up at him confidingly. (This was a neat trick, as she was a good bit taller than he was.)

"Oh, *there* you are!" she gushed, "I'm so pleased to run into you. We're all so excited about the big conference! I've been networking, and I'm pretty sure all the new and promising young authors will be there."

EDITORS' NOTE: We'll call the young man Mr. Brown for now. His hair is brown and his suit and shoes are brown and he doesn't really have enough personality to warrant a name with more character. (If you reading this are named Brown, we mean no offense.)

"The authors aren't all exactly *young*," murmured Mr. Brown.

"Well, there's a range of ages. But they're new on the *scene*," Deandra explained kindly. *I must* not *sound condescending,* she thought. *It would be* fatal *at this juncture.*

Second only to her clothing, hair, and make-up, her literary career meant everything to her.

Sage was starting to feel invisible, which was slightly annoying as he was the founder of the Post-Modernist Minimalist Neo-Symbolist Pseudo-Realist School of Literature that all this fuss was about.

"Which authors do we have, do you know?" asked Deandra, still with that absurd confiding air, designed to flatter.

Sage was getting a bit tired of her. She was pretty, yes, but highly artificial, and her constant acting and posturing were getting old. She was the exact opposite of Ruby, who was utterly natural and unselfconscious, qualities which only added to her rugged beauty.

Sage missed Ruby a lot and tried hard not to think about her, having no idea where on earth, or off it, she might be and when or if she was ever coming back. She was his desert rose, and both had believed their bond to be eternal, at least he had *thought* so, though they still hadn't gotten around to getting married. His old insecurity came back; maybe she was tired of waiting and had just left. He felt a wave of self-pity. Couldn't she have left a note?

Sage shook himself. This was ridiculous! He abruptly and purposefully wrenched his train of thought onto a different track.

Who was this Brown guy anyway? He didn't *look* like anybody special. In fact, he was consummately boring.

"And you might want to remind Mr. Sage which books each of them wrote," said Deandra, butting into Sage's thoughts.

With a dramatic flourish, Mr. Brown produced a list of books, authors, and subschools within the Post-Modernist Minimalist Neo-Symbolist Pseudo-Realist School of Literature.

Sage studied it, his appalment (appalledness?) growing by the second. (These are surely newly invented words, but tough beans, he needed them!)

This is what he saw.

BOOKS & DIVISIONS & AUTHORS

Clawdia Fanghorn and the Alligator King I-III The Pizza Pie's Wife The Story of Gerund	Heaving Bodice Romance Division Heaving Bodice Romance Division Heaving Bodice Romance Division	Deandra Hollendaise
Monday, Will You Marry Me?	Heaving Bodice Romance Division	Lydia Larchwood
The Girl with the Funny Name	Young and Restless YA Division	Lydia Larchwood
Pat the Cat	Precocious Kids Division	Lydia Larchwood
The Snove	Literary Fiction Division	Felicity Hagedorn
What's in a Name?	Literary Fiction Division	Felicity Hagedorn
The Forget-About-It Trilogy *OR* The Dinosaur Trilogy	Creation, Evolution & Metaphysics Division (Parts 1 & 2) Hardboiled Detective Division (Part 3)	Halycon Sage (Included in *The Book of Squidly Light*)
Puppy for the Defense! Or the Prosecution ...	Legal Eagle & Magical Realism Division	Gabriel Redborne
Baraboo Bartholomew, Fur Trapper with a Heart	Sensitive Macho Dude Division (Western)	Wade Garnette

Sage looked at Mr. Brown inquiringly.

"Do you want me to do something about this?" he asked in carefully noncommittal tones.

The man *beamed*. That was the only word for it. "*Do* something? Why yes, we want you to be Keynote Speaker. After all, the whole thing started with *you*. But what talent you have inspired! Look at some of these books."

He held out a number of what looked like pamphlets. Well, to be fair, there were no facilities for binding anymore. At least there was still a stapler. And staples, till they ran out.

Maybe the blacksmith could make some more, thought Sage, momentarily escaping the heavy and unwanted responsibility about to descend on his head.

EDITORS' NOTE: *The Story of Gerund*, a real dog, will not be appearing at this conference, but is merely included as part of Deandra Hollendaise's cannon. The only clever thing *in* it is the protagonist's name, which combines the names Edmund and Gerald. The remainder rests on a stupid pun about Parts of Speech, which no one would understand anyway.

"Okay, give me the shortest ones," said Sage, hoping to get out of this as painlessly as possible. Mr. Brown passed him two of the small, stapled mini-novels and he shuffled the top one to the bottom, having already read it twice, once just now and once in an alternate reality. It was *Baraboo Bartholomew, Fur Trapper with a Heart*. He looked at the other one.

The Pizza Pie's Wife, by Deandra Hollendaise, of course. He groaned softly. Was there no escaping this woman? Here is what he read.

<u>THE PIZZA PIE'S WIFE</u>
by Deandra Hollendaise
Preface

Deandra Hollendaise would not be beaten. Nevertheless, she persisted. In her ever more frequent forays to the library, she had noticed many books titled *The _____'s Wife*. Observing their popularity, she decided to write one of her own.

The Pizza Pie's Wife

It was hard being married to a pizza pie. No one really understood, and he could not entirely meet her needs. Yet sometimes, with his deep scent of tomato and oregano filling her nostrils, she felt that he utterly fulfilled her deepest longings.

He was a self-renewing pizza pie. Consumed each day, he was back again the next, his mozzarella gleaming with olive oil, his crust as firm and crisp as ever.

They went out together—he could sprout little legs when he so desired—and the odd looks could not quite spoil her pleasure in his company.

What the pizza pie himself thought about the arrangement, no one ever knew. From the spring in his step and the sparkle in his eye (???!), he appeared to be quite content.

The End

Postscript

She had exercised a modest restraint, knowing that Dry Creek Gulch was full of prudes, but she really thought her novel could have been a bit steamier.

Afterword

Deandra was not wrong. These below are all real books.

The Clockmaker's Wife
The Time Traveler's Wife
The Millionaire's Wife
The Winemaker's Wife
The Poet's Wife
The Tea Planter's Wife
The Engineer's Wife
The Tiger's Wife
The Vicar's Wife
My Husband's Wife

Sage handed the two little manuscripts back without comment, looking again at the list of authors. He noticed that the mini-novel he had previously seen was written by a Sensitive Macho Dude.

If it hadn't been for the town-encircling barrier imposed by the Squidren (or maybe by someone else now, since the Squidren vehemently denied continuing it), he would have jumped back on No-Name Stupid and escaped once again into the wide-open spaces of the familiar and welcoming desert.

CHAPTER ELEVEN

SAGE'S IMAGINARY AUTHOR

Dateline: Minneapolis, Minnesota, 2024 C.E.

Imaginary author Karima had been wanting to clean out the garage for a long time; it was piled high with junk, much of which was not hers. But knowing she would never in a million years get around to it, she had turned the task over to Deandra Hollendaise. The latter *also* being imaginary, there was some doubt as to whether she would do anything about it either, but at least Karima could stop worrying about it.

Deandra pushed the light-up rectangular button that was supposed to raise the creakily unreliable garage door. The door groaned uncertainly as though it were being asked an unreasonable favor. It began to rise, which took a while, but her luck held for once and the door remained open rather than initiating its usual majestic up-and-down minuet.

Deandra pulled out the enormous bucket of vinegar and rusty tools that had been soaking for approximately four years and hauled it over to the big garbage bin that was picked up weekly.

She moved a bunch of ugly folding chairs and some other nonsense, wishing Karima hadn't yielded to the unspoken scorn of a housemate and given away the two 1950s outdoor chaise lounges, made of light metal tubing and pink and turquoise plastic strips, which she and Karima had both loved.

After hauling out another ton of useless junk (and some vitally important papers including Karima's mother's lost novel), Deandra found what she had actually been looking for. The old *time machine* was dented and slightly rusty, but she was pretty sure it would still work.

The psychic link between Karima and Halycon Sage—both writers and one having made up the other, though the matter of who had come first has never been conclusively determined—was always operative, whether or not either was consciously aware of it.

In some version of that very moment, Sage was aboard the SquidShip conversing with a third author, Rupert Griffin, who was also CEO of UnVirtual Time

Travel ("We *take* you there!"). The partly imaginary SquidShip was a convenient meeting place since both were familiar with it and it could be conjured up instantly from wherever they happened to be. And the Squidren did not seem to mind their presence.

"You might as *well*," continued Griffin, leaning across the table and pointing his finger toward Halycon Sage as they sipped their coffee. (The culinary skills of the remaining SquidShip Nanobots had improved wonderfully; the coffee was delicious and so were the sandwiches.) "You haven't got anything *else* to do."

Sage was mildly offended. "I have *so*. Why only recently I cut up all the apples for a pie ..." Well, that was just pathetic. He started again. "There's the bow hunting to be done, and *no*," he held up his hand in the same policeman-type gesture Preisczech had used, indicating *stop right there*. "I do *not* trust Vasselschnauzer and Mr. too-big-for-his-britches Anthony Buzzard to take care of it themselves. So don't even start. They *need* me!"

Griffin knew, as did Sage himself in his better moments, that Anthony and Basil could head up the hunting teams just fine, that there were plenty of people available to do all the other work, that a new Post-Modernist Minimalist Neo-Symbolist Pseudo-Realist novel was not a pressing need at this time, and further that, with no new input to liven up his literary output, Sage himself was growing a little stale.

"You've got to get *out*," said Griffin making that annoying pointing gesture again. Sage briefly imagined his horse No-Name Stupid biting Griffin's finger. "There just isn't anything for you to do in Dry Creek Gulch right now. Ruby's gone ..."

Suddenly they were somewhere else but not too far away. (This kind of thing happened a lot due to the instability which so concerned Dry Creek Gulch's scientific community.) Sage looked out the clear, sunlit window of the new annex to the Dirty Dog Canis Fidelis Cafe, Bar, Grill, Party Room, and Gathering Space—the stupid name seemed to get longer every week and those who thought they were funny kept adding to it.

Sage didn't *want* to go anywhere! What he loved best, except for Ruby of course, was right here: clear, wide open spaces with mountains in the background, dry land and sagebrush shading into pine trees, willows along the little river that snaked away in the distance. The fresh, light wind coming through the open door brought the smell of sagebrush and pine and willow and desert dust, to him the smell of happiness and peace.

"I obviously can't get *out,*" said Sage. "*Nobody* can get out. Or have you forgotten the Wall?" he added sarcastically. He knew what Griffin was thinking, but as long as it remained unspoken, he might be able to avoid the inevitable conclusion of this conversation. They'd been dancing around this topic for weeks. But he didn't *want* to, *he didn't want to—*

Griffin slammed down his cup, ignoring the spilled coffee. "Sage, dammit, you can't weasel out of it any longer! *You've got to time travel!*"

CHAPTER TWELVE

HALYCON SAGE TALKS TO HIMSELF

Dateline: Far Future, Maybe Lydia Squidlight's Time, Maybe Not

Sage looked around. He had no idea how or why he had been time traveling. He was perfectly content in Dry Creek Gulch, though Ruby had taken off again. His various friends, up to and including author Rupert Griffin, creator and CEO of UnVirtual Time Travel, were becoming irritated with his lack of productive accomplishment in any sphere.

The different Sages who had shown up so confusingly as to make the real, involuntarily time-traveling Halycon Sage utter an actual swear word were here again, sitting around in the amphitheater, give or take a few. Now as he blinked into consciousness there, they were apparently discussing his imaginary author, some with derision, some with a degree of respect.

NARRATING SAGE: So, Karima's big life question, which colors and informs everything else, which she started thinking about as a kid and has been pondering ever since ...

WISEGUY SAGE (aside to another Sage): Pinkie, are you pondering what I'm pondering?[16]

NARRATING SAGE: Actually, ever since she read *The Caine Mutiny* at age twelve ...

WISEGUY SAGE (groaning): Oh man, here we go again!

NARRATING SAGE: So, this kind of hapless or feckless or some other kind of something-less protagonist is on a U.S. Navy destroyer minesweeper during WW2 in the Pacific Theatre.

WISEGUY SAGE: Fascinating. Here's Mr. History with the Wayback Machine.[17] I'm so excited.

IRRELEVANT SAGE: Why do they call it a theatre anyway?

NARRATING SAGE: And this ensign, Willie Keith, is sitting on the deck with the guys and they're having "ice cream with chocolate sauce."

WISEGUY SAGE: That's called "a sundae" in modern parlance. Keep up.

WORD-OBSESSED SAGE: Yeah, but why isn't it spelled S-u-n-d-a-y? And anyway, we're *post*-modern now. *You* keep up!

---

16 From the inspired *Pinkie and the Brain* cartoon show, not to be missed.
17 Referencing Mr. Peabody and Sherman, not the modern internet thing.

The real Sage reflected that these pseudo-Sages were even more annoyingly nit-picky and easily distracted than he was himself.

NARRATING SAGE: And he's feeling guilty about eating dessert on the ship while they can see Marines being blown up on the beach. Says the sauce seems "kind of luxurious." To which another character responds, "So don't eat your ice cream."

BORED SAGE: Is this going somewhere?

NARRATING SAGE: Well, it got Karima worrying about whether it was okay to enjoy yourself while others were suffering.

RADICAL REVOLUTIONARY SAGE (dismissively): Definitely First World Problems!

REASONABLE SAGE: But somebody is always suffering, so by that logic no one on Planet Earth could ever have any fun at all.

INTERRUPTING SQUID: Or anywhere else in the Multiverse!

NARRATING SAGE: Actually, she first thought about this when she was around six at the family dinner table, the one and only time her mother said, "You should eat your food, children in China are starving." Karima had replied snottily, "Well, send it to *them*, then!"

RADICAL REVOLUTIONARY SAGE: More bourgeois nonsense from someone with too much time on their hands.

NARRATING SAGE: But she was only half being a wise-guy; the other half was sincerely wondering if she could send her leftover mashed potatoes or whatever to the hungry kids in China and if that would help them. After a little reflection (later, by herself), she concluded it would cost more to send the stuff than it would be worth to anybody.

She's more informed now, but she hasn't changed very much. She still wishes she could send the delicious food her life partner cooks to Gaza.

REAL SAGE: Where's that?

SOME OTHER SAGE: Oh, right, you're from the 1990s, aren't you?

NARRATING SAGE: So, the way she finally formulates this as a kid: Would it be better if everyone in the world got two pairs of blue cotton pajamas and three bowls of rice a day *but that was it* or if people were still starving and suffering horribly but great art and music and architecture and scholarship and museum stuff and so forth existed.[18] Was the planet-wide, centuries-long accumulation of beauty and wisdom worth the agony of people with *nothing*—

REGULAR SAGE: So what did she decide?

NARRATING SAGE: She didn't, she's still trying to figure it out. In her spare time, of which she has none because of writing these books and still trying to save the world no matter how ridiculous her efforts have proven so far.

WORD OBSESSED SAGE: "Proven," an old fashioned past tense, I *like* that.

---

18 Yes, yes, embarrassing outdated stereotype, we know. These thoughts were from the 1950s.

ECCLESIASTICAL SAGE: Here endeth the lesson. The interdimensional chat with attendant quibbling is ended. Go in peace.

CHAPTER THIRTEEN

MEET SOME AUTHORS

Dateline: The Amorphous Present of the Previous Novels

About 20 miles from the center of Dry Creek Gulch lived a little girl, all alone. Well, we'll have to qualify that a bit. She was not actually a little girl anymore though she still felt like one; she had recently turned twelve. And she was not quite alone either. She had some animal friends, not pets exactly, but shy desert creatures drawn by her restful, quiet kindliness.

She was an unusual girl, not modern in any way and quite unworldly. Having been partially raised by an eccentric great aunt and uncle who had no television, let alone internet access, she was not only undisturbed by the collapse of modern technology, she had not even noticed it. And because they were preppers—eccentricity doesn't necessarily make one a fool—she had everything she needed to sustain life in reasonable comfort.

She'd been raised at times by these relatives and at other times by her adoring father, a scholar who also, like her uncle, was something of a hermit. His house beyond Dry Creek Gulch contained a floor-to-ceiling library with books in many languages: books on history and sociology, philosophy and religion, political theory and linguistics and cultural studies, books by authors like Franz Fanon and Noam Chomsky and Illan Pappe. But the girl herself preferred fiction, of which there was also a sizeable collection.

She was an odd girl. When her father failed to reappear from a post-Event foraging expedition, she calmly waited through the weeks and months, certain that he would return. (He eventually did, but that is beyond the scope of this story.)

She had everything she needed not only for her body, but for her mind and heart and spirit. She had books to read, an infinite-seeming desert to walk in, sagebrush and pine trees and a hidden hot spring for bathing. And with the company of a desert hare, a desert tortoise, and various birds, lizards and chipmunks, she was not lonely. Besides all this, she had a passion, an avocation that kept her busy. The girl was a writer.

But even out here, all alone and absorbed in her work, the land, and her animal friends, she eventually noticed that things had changed.

No cars passed by anymore. There had never been many, but *few* is different from *none*. Also, no planes flew overhead, and the night sky seemed darker and the stars more brilliant. Various light-giving objects had apparently burned out or been removed.[19]

Though the girl was quite satisfied with her quiet but enormously fulfilling existence, a strange desire began to grow within her, the desire to have someone actually read her work. And also, perhaps, the long dormant desire for the company of other humans re-emerged. So gradually, in stages, she implemented a new plan, careful and shy as a tortoise peeking out of its shell.

She was a good walker, and by stages, stopping to rest under the occasional shade trees and cliff sides, she eventually came to Dry Creek Gulch, to Main Street, and to The Dirty Dog.

As she was inconspicuous, quietly dressed and modestly looking down or away, nobody noticed her. She read the announcement on the bulletin board about the upcoming literary conference of the Post-Modernist Minimalist Neo-Symbolist Pseudo-Realist School of Literature, apparently a great event, unrivaled in the post Event reality, as far as anyone knew.

Being a writer, she immediately decided to submit some of her work, which, fortunately, she had brought with her. Her mini-novels were light and easy to carry,

---

19 Ah, Preisczech. Evidently the scientist had felt there was too much light pollution and human-made junk both on earth and in space and had gotten rid of it, all the artifacts and technologies he considered dangerous, unnecessary, or just annoying to himself and everyone else in town.

and she had more hand-written copies of them at home. So, she tacked them up on the community bulletin board in the bar, cafe, whatever it was, and again, nobody noticed her.

There are two more things you need to know about her before we close this introductory episode. First, her name. You may have wondered why we keep awkwardly referring to her as "the girl," but it was for the enjoyment of a Big Reveal right now. Well, a mini-Big Reveal. Her name, which you have encountered on Mr. Brown's list of novelists presenting at the conference, is Lydia Larchwood: author of *Pat the Cat*, *The Girl with the Funny Name*, and *Monday, Will You Marry Me?* So, as you can see, her work has been fully accepted and in fact is much appreciated by the scarce but enthusiastic literati of Dry Creek Gulch.

The second thing you should know is that, while no one noticed her, she herself did notice someone. Boys had not come her way before. Indeed, practically nobody had come her way. But over by the jukebox stood a boy. The first thing she noticed was his hair, which was black and fell around his face in loose curls. At the moment he was laughing at something a companion had said, and his black eyes sparkled with intelligence and kindly merriment.

He was tall and well set up, slim but strong-looking, maybe seventeen years of age. His skin was light brown, to Lydia a lovely color. His hands were works of art, strong and graceful, and everything else about him seemed just as it should be. She had almost never seen a boy, but he reminded her of the princes in some of her father's books, the ones who were good and kind and modest and brave and all that stuff. When the laugh ended, his face assumed a thoughtful seriousness, which seemed habitual with him.

She noticed all this before she noticed his clothing, something else she had not come across before. He wore a long white garment she would almost have called a dress, but he wore it with a masculine ease. And really, she had almost no knowledge of how modern people dressed. (The heroine of her book, *The Girl with the Funny Name,* shared her near-complete ignorance of modern dress and habits. This can happen to those brought up by eccentrics.)

Quietly, she watched. He stood with a little group of people: a small, scruffy bearded man, a towering Black man whose sudden smile revealed a shining gold tooth, and an older couple who, from their resemblance to the young man and his affectionate yet deferential attitude toward them, she thought might be his parents. His face was thoughtful, sensitive, and kind.

As though he felt her gaze upon him, he suddenly looked up. Their eyes locked for a moment, a deep unspoken meeting. Then he flashed a reassuring smile, as if he understood her embarrassment, and she quickly looked away. *In a few more years, who knows?* she thought.

∽

Wade Garnette was not a happy camper and this was more than metaphorical. He was a camper, literally, and at this moment, he was not happy! Like several other characters in our chronicle, Mr. Garnette had various neurotic tendencies. (Do they even use that word anymore? No matter.)

Being a Sensitive Macho Dude, he had begun to fret about the health and welfare of his protagonist, Baraboo Bartholomew. Just like Halycon Sage with his made-up author Karima, or Karima with her made-up author Halycon Sage, he knew perfectly well that the character was not real and therefore could not be distressed or injured, either emotionally or physically.

But just as with the two examples above, Bartholomew had begun to assume a sort of quasi-reality for his creator, and the author was worried. What was the guy supposed to *eat?* A trapper who couldn't kill an animal would surely die out here; you can't eat sagebrush and manzanita!

Of course a fictional character could not become distressingly hungry, so what was the author fussing about? He looked nervously over his shoulder as a western hare bounded swiftly down the mountain, scattering dust and little rocks.

He was not a vegetarian. If he could catch that hare, skin it, and cook it over an open fire, he could feed it to Bartholomew and assure his character's survival. But this idea was absurd for more reasons than Baraboo's fictional status. For Garnette had about as much chance of catching that hare as he had of joining the new Squidish expedition to the Farther Galaxy. Which is to say, zero!

Even if he caught it, skinning it would turn his stomach and break his heart. Like the two mutually created authors above, he shared much of his character's personality, and though he was not a vegetarian, the less the meat he ate looked like an animal, the better he liked it. He favored hotdogs, salami, and packaged sliced turkey. Though a big fan of fried and breaded chicken nuggets, the thought of cutting up a raw chicken made him sick.

He continued down the mountain toward Dry Creek Gulch, subliminally fussing and worrying about his vulnerable and hapless character. Perhaps Baraboo could take up some other profession, snake charming for instance. There were plenty of rattlers out here to give the story verisimilitude,[20] though they were far from charming.

At least when Wade Garnette finally got to town, he'd have a place to stay. Because, though he'd heard the Dirty Dog did not rent rooms, there was a place called The House of Cats that looked like an old western saloon, and he was pretty sure he could put up there.

---

20 Or, as rendered by lawyer Cantrip in Sarah Caudwell's hilarious novels, "verysmellitude."

CHAPTER FOURTEEN

A SIP OF ARABIC

Dateline: Minneapolis 2024

Imaginary author Karima was a perpetual Arabic student. Some of those who knew her might have wondered how she was teaching beginning Arabic at Jawahir School of Dance in the 1990s, but in 2024 she was studying Arabic on Duolingo. This seems a bit incongruous, but both Karima and the Arabic language, at least to an outside observer, are incongruous in many ways.

Some of the sentences made Karima laugh. "I like my lion, but I do not like her lion," or "My cat has a question, Professor." And, "My aunt is weird, but we do not hate her."

Her favorite so far, belying the absurd stereotype of humorless Arabs, was, "Every cat needs a pink dress." Whoever wrote these things was clearly having fun.

Other sentences, using *ghareeb* (weird, غريب), translated as, "You are a very weird teacher, Mike," or "You are a weird Jordanian engineer, Reem." Presumably these sentences would never be used in real life, but they made good teaching tools and building blocks.

This method of imprinting a limited number of nouns, verbs, and adjectives on the students until they were ready to move forward was very congenial to her learning style. Students were allowed to soak in the stuff till it made sense. (This is also how babies learn language.)

The adjectives currently being reinforced translated as famous, important, large, new, weird, and hungry. The word for hungry is pronounced ja-*WAAN*. There were many sentences such as, "*Ana Umar wa ana muhandis jawaan,*" "*Anta mutarjima jawaan jidan, ya 'Ali,*" and "*Ana wa binti jawaan jidan!*" which translate variously as "I am Umar and I am a hungry engineer," "You are a very hungry translator, Ali," and "My daughter and I are very hungry."

Karima, who could become unconscious of other contexts while pursuing one particular line of thought, was *pleased* for these diverse hungry people because surely they were about to satisfy their hunger with a big plate of falafel, yellow rice, tomatoes, and other good stuff, or maybe a giant sandwich, sometimes rendered as *sahnd-weetsh* (ساندويتش"). According to her Sudanese Arabic professor of many years ago, some country's Arabic Language Board, resisting innovation, had once advised calling it "a piece of bread with another piece of bread with something fresh in between." This was eventually rejected as being too long, too cumbersome, and too *ghareeb*. The professor also inquired "What if it's a *stale* sandwich?"

But suddenly, *oh!* The historical context of the moment came crashing down upon her. What if these various engineers, translators, teachers, professors and their husbands and wives and babies did not *have* a sandwich? What if they had no falafel, no rice, no tomatoes. What if they were eating leaves or animal feed or nothing at all? Abruptly, the word *jawaan* took on a very different meaning.

CHAPTER FIFTEEN

TIME TRAVEL ON PURPOSE

A few days after his talk with Rupert Griffin, Sage sighed and decided to make the leap. After all, they'd been foreshadowing it long enough, through several books if his memory served him correctly. And the only time travelers so far had been a villain plotting to destroy the Earth and the Blue Thread Team which followed him, trying to undo the damage. And of course, Rupert Griffin, creator of UnVirtual Time Travel ("We *take* you there!") And recently Sage himself, in his involuntary trips to some unimaginable far future.

As a writer, Sage could see that this potential cornucopia of meanings, adventures, and new plot twists had been sadly underutilized.

"Hmmmm …" Mumbling under his breath, he sifted through various periods he might be interested in.

"Late 1100s to early 1200s, a fascinating time." Though he didn't know much about specific years, the whole long Medieval era intrigued him. *I would have felt at home there*, he thought. A good place for a wandering minstrel or storyteller or knight errant. He had always been a bit errant, erring into odd places and now, it appeared, into odd times as well.

"1492. Or 1620. Meh." Though perhaps he could do something to stop the problem before it began, as he'd done in his first book, *101 Cows: A Novel*. He had a quick vision of himself standing on the seashore, yelling at an approaching ship or ships, "*PLAGUE! RUN!!!* Run for your *LIVES!!!*" But for his first venture into other elsewhens, he wanted something less participatory, more observational.

"2024." Strange historical changes and anachronisms were happening there, things that would be interesting to an amateur historian such as himself. Very amateur, but also very intrigued by the ways the craziest things came to be accepted as normal *(Doesn't everybody shrink heads?)* and also the way certain behaviors and attitudes came round and round again like a particular spotted horse on a merry-go-round.

At the thought of horses he lost concentration for a moment. Where was No-Name Stupid? He didn't really feel like *himself* without Stupid. But there would be time for that, probably all the time in the world. It would be interesting to see what Stupid, or the various versions of him if such existed, had been getting up to.

There was something of historic significance going on in Gaza 2024, though he wasn't quite sure what. A major shift, something that could bring on either an actual and final apocalypse[21] or a new birth for humanity, the creatures, and Planet Earth herself. He didn't know much about the details, but his unerring intuitive sense told him that this was one of the great branchings of human history, and that it could go either way. It would certainly be interesting, and perhaps he could help somehow.

Suddenly Preisczech was there. "*No,*" he cried in sheer, hair-standing-on-end horror. *Noooooo! Not 2024! Sage, come baaaaaaaack.*

It was too late.

---

21 Not like the baby apocalypse he had already participated in and, with the help of his friends, narrowly averted. See *The Book of Squidly Light*, volume two of The Sage Chronicles.

CHAPTER SIXTEEN

HALYCON SAGE TALKS TO HIMSELF AGAIN

REGULAR SAGE: I'm not very comfortable with this. What's this Gaza stuff I'm hearing about? Floating into my consciousness at odd times, I mean. Some kind of bleed-through.

WISEGUY SAGE: Bleed-through, that's a good word for it!

UNIDENTIFIED SAGE: I hope you don't think you're being funny!

WISEGUY SAGE: No, no, I was never more serious.

REGULAR SAGE: I have no idea what you guys are talking about!

NARRATING SAGE: Oh, you will. You will. Some of us seem to be from a time in your future. I mean, when you're not in this Indeterminate In-between Space.

REGULAR SAGE: So you know things I don't? And how it's all going to come out?

UNIDENTIFIED SAGE: Yes!

ANOTHER SAGE: No!

NARRATING SAGE: Maybe … You're going to go there. This *Gaza*. Or you've just been there. It's hard to talk about sequence in the In-Between Space.

REGULAR SAGE: Where is it anyway? Huxley wrote a book called *Eyeless in Gaza*, but I've never read it.

WISEGUY SAGE: Neither has Karima.

REGULAR SAGE: If you're implying that we're the same person, that stupid rumor was debunked years ago. So quit it!

WISEGUY SAGE: Well, she'd better read it before she mentions it and makes a fool of herself. Again.[22]

REGULAR SAGE: So, that messed up guy isn't still president, right?

UNIDENTIFIED SAGE: No.

ANOTHER SAGE: Yes.

NARRATING SAGE: *Again*. Remember, we're all from different times.

SAGE: But what about now?

ECCLESIASTICAL SAGE (ironically): *Now?* It's *all* now.

This was getting out of hand.

REGULAR SAGE: So, I'm finally going to time travel in a big way? Besides this crazy far future and In-Between Space stuff, I mean?

---

22 We note after briefly researching that book that it has nothing whatsoever to do with anything here.

ECCLESIASTICAL SAGE: All in good time my friend. My
brother. Myself.

REGULAR SAGE: *(Wanting to say something mildly sarcastic
about the hokeyness of this, but unable to think of
anything.)* See you guys later.

He rises, nods politely, and walks out of the
auditorium.

CHAPTER SEVENTEEN

A PEEK AT THE PUPPYVERSE

Another transition: Before we meet Gabriel Redborne's character Attorney Edwin Puppy in real life (i.e., Dry Creek Gulch), we're going to share some of *Puppy for the Defense* right here so you'll have a sense of who exactly we're dealing with. Further chapters (or episodes if it's a streaming show) will doubtless be included as readings when we attend the First Annual Literary Conference of the Post-Modernist Minimalist Neo-Symbolist Pseudo-Realist School of Literature. Here goes!

Puppy for the Defense!
Or, the Prosecution …

by Gabriel Redborne

Chapter One

Edwin Puppy got all the bad jobs. Today it was a Document Dump. Boxes and boxes and boxes of it, sent over from the prosecutor's office. Puppy had always thought the defense were the good guys. He hadn't reckoned on *corporate* defense, those sleazy weasels, whose job was to help clients get out of paying their obligations.

This was a worker's compensation case based on something called a repetitive stress injury—an injury that happens, not all at once, but through the repetition of a stressful action, sometimes over a period of years. Mr. Davis, a miner of some type, was clearly injured and had clearly been injured on the job. But since two different insurance companies had covered his employer over the man's working life, each was trying to blame the injury on the other. Nobody wanted to pay, just like always.

Puppy looked at the towering boxes of documents and sighed.

"Man up, Puppy!" said senior partner Silvaneous Panther, who never seemed to do any work, but smoked a really big cigar.

But Edwin Puppy could not man up. Because he was a puppy!

THE END

Puppy for the Defense!
Or, the Prosecution ...

Chapter Two

Edwin Puppy had a problem. He wanted to work for the *good* guys. This meant that he wanted sometimes to prosecute, and sometimes to defend. As had been explained to young Mr. Puppy, a trial lawyer is either a prosecutor or a defender. You couldn't switch back and forth. This seemed so unfair! Puppy thought he should be able to represent the side he thought was *right*. The other lawyers laughed and shook their heads, but Puppy remained unconvinced.

It occurred to him that he could work for both a noble defense firm and a fearless prosecutor's office, though of course neither could know about the other. This would take considerable skill, but young Mr. Puppy was optimistic, clever, and full of energy.

Sifting quickly through the mountains of meaningless files, he began evolving his clever plan. He would've thought twice about this, had he known where it would lead.

"For want of a nail the shoe was lost, for want of a shoe the horse was lost. For want of a horse, the rider was lost. For want of a rider the message was lost. For want of a message the battle was lost. For want of a battle the kingdom was lost. All for the want of a horseshoe nail."

Edwin Puppy was about to become the little piece of grit that caused the loss of the first nail and the beginning of the chain reaction. If Mr. Panther ever found out, Mr. Panther would bite him.

EDITORS' NOTE: The firm in question is called Horse, Fish, Panther & Puppy. All but Puppy are senior partners. Why he is a *name* partner without being a *senior* partner, and usually stuck in the mail room, is something we may never know.

THE END

Puppy for the Defense!
Or, the Prosecution ...

Chapter Three

E dwin Puppy thought out his plot, the bare bones of his clever plan.[23] Slowly and carefully he developed it, modeling himself on his heroes from legal novels and T.V. shows.[24]

---

23 And he was very fond of bones.
24 Mike from *Suits,* and the firm of Upshaw, Parker & Lane from John Grisham's *The Rooster Bar.* Nobody from *Boston Legal,* which he found deeply shocking.

He would have a secret name that he would use in the prosecutor's office. He would be Edward Youngdog. No one would ever guess that they were the same person because he would wear a *disguise*.

The basic concept was an idea whose time had come, and in the Alternate Universe where technology still worked, it was almost immediately picked up by a big streaming service, which parlayed Mr. Puppy's travails and adventures into a weekly series of many episodes. It was rumored that a second season was under development.[25]

THE END

---

25 Karima, who advised on this project or was connected with it somehow, saw two other legal shows whose heroes' personalities, looks, and attitudes toward the law were remarkably similar to Puppy's, but swears she had the idea before she saw them. She was told she was just "plugged into the zeitgeist."

CHAPTER EIGHTEEN

THE OTHER SIDE OF AN OLD FRIEND

Jenny didn't often think about her previous life. She was too busy and happy. As the premier cook and baker of the town, not only a good plain cook but able to produce food from many Earth cuisines on a whim, she actually had more trouble concealing her methods than *making* the stuff. Bread was easier because she rose very early to do her baking, hopefully before others would come snooping around. If they did, there were methods.

She worked hard at making the lovely food—cooking, canning, drying, pickling—and giving afternoon classes enabling interested others to do the same. Some of these Earthlings were quite talented that way.

It was an enormous relief to focus on the micro level required by Earth life. One thing at a time, methodically.

Making sure each foot touched the ground with every step, neither too lightly nor slamming into it, had required a bit of practice.

TechieSquid had been a help, and that help had been needed. Because focusing down small enough had been quite a trick for someone used to navigating the Multiverse in a form resembling enormous, flashing squares of light, glasslike and paper-thin, intersecting at impossible angles, and colored brilliantly magenta, turquoise, purple, blue, or clear.[26]

Earth life was so little and sweet, and she was still devoted to Preisczech, who knew exactly who and what she was and still returned her love with an answering devotion.

Ruby had been a help too. Jenny had shown her some secrets of the Multiverse, and Ruby, evincing no surprise, had taken to navigating space-time as handily as she rode a motorcycle or handled a horse. Ruby was never rattled by anything, and she had always been good at practical things. If there was anything to complain about with Ruby, it was her tendency to disappear too suddenly and stay away too long.

This was beginning to cause comment among the Dry Creek Gulchians. But it was nothing pressing, and nothing that couldn't be handled. She'd have to have a

---

26 We can get no closer to describing Jenny's actual form, which predated even her appearance as the Squid Empress. She hid some of her colors from the conservative Squids, who still rejected the higher range of magenta, purple, and violet. This prejudice had caused problems before, and easily could again.

talk with Ruby when the newly trained multidimensional traveler got back. (For she had taken off again almost immediately after dropping in for breakfast.)

This literary conference though, now *that* was worrying, taking up people's time and attention just when everyone needed to be laser focused, unplugged from any distraction. Because a crisis point was coming, a big one. If you were a Squid or some other sensitive, you could feel it in the air.

Jenny had picked up a slight human habit of fretting and worrying. At first it seemed well aligned with her human character, which after all needed to have some negative attributes, but now it had a tendency to manifest on its own even when she didn't want it too. *Rats,* thought Jenny, echoing Sophie.

CHAPTER NINETEEN

SOMETIMES ARABIC LESSONS CAN HURT

"How is there no dessert?"

"Who does not want warm bread?"

"No, he does not like kibbeh and falafel."

"My sister does not want tabbouleh and kabab."

"I do not like juice and I do not want juice."

"My friend Ali does not want tea."

"You do not like kabab, but you want kabab today, correct?"

"Palestine is an important and historic place."

"I want to travel to Palestine."

"I am from a large Palestinian city."

— from the language learning app Duolingo

GAZA 2024

Sage looked around. He'd taken a moment during his time jump to stop off and do a little research, inhaling a block of knowledge.

There was supposed to be a village here and a city nearby. Date palms and olive groves and farms, animals grazing; colorful houses large and small; beautiful mosques, churches and museums. In the city were prestigious universities with huge, magnificent buildings and manicured grounds, gathering places for the learned and for aspiring scholars, including a gracious campus of Al-Azhar, the famous Islamic university and one of the oldest surviving universities in the world.

And a lovely seacoast. (*Sahal al-bahr*, thought Karima, who was semi-consciously catching a bit of this while doing other things.) Fresh fish, blue-green water and white sand beaches, charming restaurants, families laughing and swimming in their beautiful homeland.

It sounded like heaven to Halycon Sage, who had always loved the Mediterranean—*al-bahr al-abyad al-mutawasit*, the White Middle Sea—though he'd been there only in imagination.

"Palestine is a beautiful country," remarked one of Karima's Arabic dialogues.

But where was it? Sage saw rubble, rubble, and more rubble. Crumbled concrete interspersed with twisted metal and ruined bricks and boards. There was a terrible smell of rot and fetid water.

There were people there, crying and wailing. Smoke and fire could be seen in the sky and on the ground, in the near and in the far. There was blood everywhere, and bodies and body parts. A man cried out, *"Why, why? He was my son! He had done nothing!"*

Sage heard the siren of an ambulance, and it came near enough for him to see it clearly, bearing the logo of some international aid organization. At least whatever was going on, the international community was there to help. But the thing couldn't get through, because the road was gone. Then an explosion came from the sky, and the ambulance was gone too. *Problem solved*, thought Sage with a bitter and heart-broken sarcasm.

From his vantage point above the road, he had seen that the ambulance was clearly marked on the roof as well as on the side, so whoever bombed it couldn't deny knowing what it was. Who would target an *ambulance?* From an *international aid organization?* It didn't make sense.

Dimly, knowledge seeped into Sage's consciousness from Karima. Newborn babies dying in incubators when the hospital's electricity was intentionally shut off. The most child amputations in the world in an area twenty-five miles long, done without anesthetic, because there *was* none. People losing two hundred relatives. (Who in the United States even *had* two hundred relatives?) The beautiful faces of artists and students, doctors and poets, children and scientists and journalists, one young woman holding her cat. All dead now. Unbearable even to see or to read about. How about living it?

A little while later … Sage was staggering around in the rubble, half in and half out of this time and place, sickened, appalled, almost unable to move. *How could this be? What has happened?*

At that moment, two ancestors of imaginary author Karima and her imaginary husband came through, speaking clearly in Sage's mind. The tall, handsome black-haired man in the beautifully tailored suit said dryly, "That'll do." This was what he used to say when he was *done*, when something entirely unacceptable had to be firmly squashed.

The white-haired woman—proper, intelligent-looking and slightly frightening—said the opposite, but it meant the same thing.

"That won't do," she said in a cold, cold voice.

And they were right.

I can travel in time, thought Sage, *and this needs to be fixed*.

His first thought was to go back in time to undo this the way they'd undone the nuclear catastrophe caused by nihilist author Neimand Kompt. He would go back to … he scanned … October 7, 2023 … no, that was not the beginning. About 17 years previous, when it became "the world's largest open-air prison"? No, that wasn't it either. Two more skips then, to 1948. A Rabbi friend had once told him, "The Jews were in a burning house.

They jumped out the widow, fell on the Palestinians, and killed them."

At this point, someone he did not know gently intervened; he heard her voice in his head. "Not the past," she said. *"The future."*

"I am from a very old Palestinian city," remarked the Duolingo language program.

Umm Nuri, also known as Leila, was baking cookies. While she still made many dishes from her Iraqi origins, she also liked making some western-derived treats, particularly the chocolate chip cookies she'd acquired from Emily and Jenny the Squid Empress.

She'd also picked up a bit of American and English music over the years and was absently humming *Oh Little Town of Bethlehem* as she laid out the second batch on a cookie sheet. It was nearing the Christians' Christmas holiday, something she felt Muslims could share in fully, since the birth of *Sayyidina Isa, alayhi salaam,* known in English as Jesus, was described in the Qur'an as well as in the Bible. In fact, his mother Mariam *radi Allahu anha,* had her own chapter, which was more than the Christians could say!

"Oh, little town of Bethlehem how still we see thee lie. Above thy deep and dreamless sleep, the silent stars go by," she sang in her sweet voice.

Leila stopped. There was something wrong, something strange in the air revealing just a hint of itself like the corner of a sheet being turned back to reveal a body underneath. *Strange image for me to have,* thought Leila, who was usually optimistic, someone who focused on beauty and the guidance of Allah. Words floated through her head.

Two-thousand-pound bombs … women and babies … filthy water or none, hospitals and schools gone … body parts … return of polio, vaccines denied … starvation as a weapon of war, violating international law. Food aide as a trap, bringing people to be shot.

The sounds and images faded. She shook herself, wondering what she had been thinking, and returned to her normal cheerful practicality.

"Above thy deep and dreamless sleep, the silent stars go by," sang Leila, sliding the last batch of cookies into the oven.

CHAPTER TWENTY

WHAT'S TRULY NEEDED

Dateline: Dry Creek Gulch, the Usual Time

Ruby Echevaria and Halycon Sage had actually been in close proximity several times recently, just barely missing each other as in some silly romantic comedy. When she popped back into existence at the Dirty Dog Cafe—we've decided to compromise on the name—he was just down the road in the SquidShip, insofar as the SquidShip could be said to have any physical location.

Twice while he was in the Indeterminate In-Between Space, she went to check for him at his little house and also went to the cave he used to frequent, the one that had served as a refrigerator for the humans and, deeper in, as a sort of cosmic movie theatre for productions put on by the Squidren.

Though in one sense they were a million years apart, in another, they were close enough to touch. Once, in fact, she was sitting on his lap if only space and not time had been considered. During this succession of near misses, each thought that the other had probably lost interest and moved on.

Ruby had even seen him once or twice eyeing Deandra with a kind of reluctant admiration, though if confronted he would have denied this hotly. Well, since they'd never actually married there was no binding obligation if one of them got bored or wanted to look elsewhere. (Neither felt this way but each thought the other did.)

Ruby and Sage missed each other terribly, but both manifested the same sort of stupid pride which allowed them no more than a casual, "Seen Sage around lately?" Or, "So Jenny, you know where Ruby is these days?"

To which Jenny had only shrugged her elegant electric blue Squid arms. The arms told the literal truth; she didn't know exactly where Ruby was, though she *did* know that she herself had sent her friend on a mission across the Multiverse. Jenny had lately encountered the old wartime expression, "Loose lips sink ships," and facing this new danger, worse than anything they'd encountered before, she thought there might be something to it.

[Timeless Pause}

Disembodied Voice: Do we really have to tell them about the Project? What a bore!

Second Voice: I think we should. We're telling them everything else, why not bring them all the way in?

[Another Timeless Pause]

First Voice: Alright, since we've already dropped some hints about the upcoming crisis point, we might as well explain a bit more. We haven't mentioned the extra-galactic mission yet, have we?

Second Voice: I don't think so. Actually, I'm not sure. Go on, you explain it.

First Voice: Well, our little band of humans, animals, Squidren, and others have staved off or reversed the end of the world twice already, but this time the danger is *worse*, and it's the belief of those in charge that every possible gift and potentiality is needed. All the physical and metaphysical weapons that have been gathered and honed, all the skills and talents that have been cultivated. In short: Everybody and everything!

And *this* time, actual physical travel is required. While these things can usually be managed through teleportation and telepathy, sometimes one actually has to *go* somewhere.

Ruby has been sent out first as a scout by Jenny the Squid Empress, but the actual expedition requires a physical vehicle to accommodate some of those who'll be going along. The SquidShip fits the bill perfectly; it's partially physical, and can become more so when the need arises.

✋

Now we shift location. Once again, just as in *The Book of Squidly Light*, Basel Vaselchnauzer sits on the SquidShip with paper and pencils listing all the things and beings that are needed.

Like the Dirty Dog Cafe, the ship has become a gathering place for meetings, luncheons, interdimensional office work and what have you. The main difference between the two locations is the ratio of Squids to humans. Other aliens sometimes drop in as well.

Basel's list includes: The SquidShip, thus the Squidren. The Black Foam Ball of Ultimate Significance, thus the Cat Fatty Lumpkin. The Cuttlefish, therefore Nuri, now well grown. Some muscle: Thus, the remnants of the Fifth Street Mofos and the Dirty Dog Boys. Technical expertise: TechieSquid and the computer geeks from the mountains, though they haven't had any computers to geek around with for a long time.

Grace, beauty, and enchantment: Thus, the dangerous and lovely Squidresses and felines currently residing at The House of Cats and—God help us—Deandra Hollendaise. The left brain: Sophie, Preisczech, and Abdurraheem. The right brain and the spirit: The Black Thread Team, comprised of Leila Umm Nuri, Halycon Sage, and Ratbone: Augustus T. Rathbone, who has a

108

streetwise worldliness that works in strange harmony with his intellectual and metaphysical gifts. Poets and visionaries: Therefore Lol Bay and No-Name Stupid.

Finally, Higher Authority. Usually those of us with the requisite energy and ingenuity can muddle along together or by ourselves, but sometimes more is needed. We already have Jenny the Squid Empress, comfortably snuggled down in her disguise which at this point fools almost nobody, but this time we also need the Adequately Magnificent Presence (referred to at the beginning of *The Way Beyond* as the Eminence) and some other intergalactic races, maybe even the *Snrrr*. Certainly the Chilidians, cynics though they are.

EDITORS' NOTE: What you are reading at this moment is a combination of Basel's terse list of objects, beings, and capacities with a bleedthrough of thoughts from various Squidren and humans who are nearby or psychically connected.

In short, the Braided Thread Teams are back! We're needed for serious world-saving again, and this time a bunch of us have to travel through hyperspace! thinks a passing Squid, delighted at the prospect.

At this very moment, turning it all over in their minds, Ruby and this anonymous Squid are having the same thought: *I certainly hope we won't need [Fill in the blank]!*

I hope we won't need Neimand Kompt! thinks Ruby, recalling dubiously the supervillain and nihilist author's change of heart after the *last* End of the World, when he broke down in tears after confronting his own evil and was given a comforting hug by Halycon Sage. But who could tell if this apparently fundamental change would *stick?* He could easily have slipped back into his old ways, couldn't he?

The Squid was contemplating the *Snrrrr*, many times voted The Most Annoying Race in the Universe. Both Ruby and the Squid shuddered, hoping fervently that their fear would not be realized. It seems unlikely to those addressing you now that either hope will be fulfilled.

Intergalactagram from Ruby: The mission must go to the Supragalactic Court of the Greater Multiverse. The only one who can help us is there. The other beings who need to be gathered are there. The remedy is there. Stop. Authentic telegrams must always say Stop. We do not know why, but TechieSquid has found this in Methods of Earth Communication 101. Stop.

CHAPTER TWENTY-ONE

MEET MORE AUTHORS

**Dateline: Dry Creek Gulch,
Same Time as Last Time.
The Convention Approaches!**

Felicity Hagedorn was a mystery. Though she had lived in Dry Creek Gulch near the center of town for about five years, nobody knew her. She seemed to have no close family, no distant relatives, no friends, no pets, no job, and no recreational activities. She only left her house and garden—yes, she *did* have a garden—to shop for occasional necessities. When she was out and about, she did not answer polite comments or meet anyone's eye. After the Event[27] she grew even more isolated. Even a fishy, rejecting stare was denied to those reaching out with some pleasantry about the weather or another bland and neutral topic.

---

27 The first averted End of the World.

What she did inside her house was a mystery, not that it was anyone's business. She had gray hair, a nondescript but slightly craggy face and appeared to be about fifty years of age. Not a pretty, well-turned-out fifty, or a sporty or self-confident fifty, or a successfully intellectual fifty, or any of those familiar variations.

She looked old before her time, like someone who had pretty much given up on everything. Yet there was a dangerous glint in her eye indicating that she did not suffer fools gladly. As with a number of those included in our chronicle, the appearance was in direct contradiction to the reality.

If her name seems familiar to you, it's because Ms. Hagedorn was another writer, author of the literary fiction works *The Snove*, and *What's in a Name?* Those evaluating authors for inclusion as conference presenters agreed that *What's in a Name?* was pretty awful, perhaps sharing a sub-genre with Deandra Hollendaise's truly terrible *The Story of Gerund*, that is, would-be witty productions centered around some pathetic and limping pun.

The committee that decided who and what would be included was unanimous on the subject of *Gerund*, but there was a split decision regarding *What's in a Name?* While everyone thought it was pretty bad, a majority of the judges thought it should be included for the two funny band names at the end. Finally, a compromise was reached, and Felicity Hagedorn was invited to read, not the whole of her new mini-novel, but the last two paragraphs.

The Snove, however, incited unbridled excitement, being, among other things, a textbook example of true Literary Fiction.

∽

There's just one more of these writers, representatives of the Post-Modernist Minimalist Neo-Symbolist Pseudo Realist School of Literature near enough to gather in Dry Creek Gulch, and that is Gabriel Redborne, an entirely different kettle of fish.

Redborne had a problem, one more complicated than those faced by the other authors, though they all had their issues, hidden or apparent. The problem was not *Puppy for the Defense! Or the Prosecution ...* which was coming along beautifully, a huge hit with millions of viewers on Petflix in the Alternate Universe. The problem was Mr. Edwin Puppy himself.

Redborne's protagonist certainly had some personal issues which you'll see in the following chapters, but these caused no difficulty for the writer; they delighted him! The problem was Mr. Puppy's uncertain status as an imaginary character, a created being, or something in between.

You may already know that several of our characters have stepped out of their fictional worlds into the real worlds of Dry Creek Gulch, the Alternate Universe, and the wider Multiverse, and certainly this creates a degree of confusion.

The most obvious case is that of Halycon Sage and Karima Vargas Bushnell. One of them had begun as a perfectly respectable fictional character but had subsequently stepped forward and claimed agency. Claimed, in fact, to have invented the other! There had even been lawsuits about it. *The Matter of Sage vs. Vargas*, and, in a nearby dimension, *The Matter of Vargas vs. Sage*.

Yet in most realities across the Multiverse they were good friends, or, at worst, merely minor irritants to each other.

Three characters whose transitions from story to reality worked out particularly well are the Appocalypse Zombie, Tarzun (the 'u' is essential) and F. Atty. Lumpkin, Esq., though Fatty's situation is by far the most complicated of the three.

F. Atty. started out as an unusually intelligent but not entirely unique EarthCat and, after transitioning to the other side, continued to display the same agency, daring, and initiative that had characterized his planetary life. He really had *three* identities: Earth Fatty, Other Side Fatty, and Fatty the Fictional Character, the last one splitting into three *further* identities: the Iraqi family's unnamed orange cat in *The Way Beyond*, the dashing hero of Sage's mini-novel *Romance for Cat and Squid*, and that redoubtable master of the courtroom, F. Atty. Lumpkin, Esq.

Fatty was one of a very few beings in Dry Creek Gulch whose psychic powers were known to affect physical reality across time, space, and possibly even from the Other Side. (See the Black Foam Ball of Ultimate Significance in *The Book of Squidly Light*.)

So, though it's delightful when characters guide and lead an author, standing up to say and do interesting things and create fresh new lines of inquiry, further claims to free will and independence can cause problems even worse than mutually contradictory assertions of who is writing whom. And Gabriel Redborne was facing just such a problem in the days leading up to the Great Literary Conference. Mr. Edwin Puppy was *off the leash!*

The problem, something we've observed with other characters, is that Puppy was not only becoming real, but was using his developing skills and talents to make an amazing amount of trouble for Mr. Gabriel Redborne.

It was one of Puppy's contentions in the lawsuit he brought against his purported author that Redborne's claim to have created him was both presumptuous and blasphemous, and that consequently, Puppy was owed a great deal of money in damages for public embarrassment, inconvenience, lost benefits and reputation, and hurt feelings.

All this naturally leads us back to …

Puppy for the Defense!
Or, the Prosecution …

CHAPTER TWENTY-TWO

THE CONTINUING ADVENTURES OF EDWIN PUPPY

**Dateline: We're Not Really Sure
As This Has Become Confusing**

**Puppy for the Defense!
Or, the Prosecution …**

Chapter Four

"**C**ome on, Puppy, let's get with it! Let's hustle!" said Panther, gliding into Puppy's little office. Senior Partner Panther himself did not hustle. He slunk, but in an elegant, high-class way. As you might imagine, Silvaneous Panther was popular among the ladies. Puppy would have been too, with his innocent dark eyes and perky face, but he was too shy and always looked away.

"New case for you, kid," said Panther, setting down a box of files. "Class action suit. Eight hundred and fifty-five miners, suing about asbestos. Or coal or something. Black lung, that's it."

Panther flicked a speck of dust from his elegant sleeve, looking at his watch as he did so. "Eight additional men are the class representatives. You're running defense."

He glided out the door as noiselessly as he had come.

With Panther safely gone, Puppy began to daydream. He imagined himself in a corner office, sitting back in a big beautiful leather chair listening to his grateful clients. He rose politely as the eight men entered the room. They were miners, part of the class action suit he had just won. *Their lung damage will be compensated now, maybe even cured,* thought the optimistic Edwin Puppy. *They'll have nice houses, the best medical care, no worries at all. And so will the other eight-hundred-and-fifty-five*, thought Puppy happily.

"Think nothing of it, gentlemen, it was my pleasure," he modestly told his erstwhile clients. And he meant it, it really was!

Defense! thought Puppy. *How wonderful!* He would defend these brave men against the unwarranted, frivolous and persecutorial lawsuit initiated by the coal company … wait, though.

Puppy rose, walked down the hall, and stuck his head in the door of the corner office of Silvaneous Panther.

"Is this *corporate defense?*" asked the horrified Puppy.

Apparently Panther was not too busy, for he was amused, rather than annoyed.

"Right on the money," said the senior partner sarcastically. "There's no getting anything by you, is there, Puppy? Sharp as a tack! No worries, though. All you'll have to do is prove that their damage was minimal: the dead ones didn't suffer much because they didn't survive that long, and the remaining ones aren't worth much because they're unskilled and stupid. Piece of cake."

Silently, Puppy returned to his office, where he sat stunned, speechless and unable to move for a full minute.

Now there was no choice! Crazy as it seemed, Edwin Puppy would have to put his plan into action!

[To be continued]

Puppy for the Defense!
Or, the Prosecution ...

Chapter Five

The first thing needful was to create the character and appearance of Edward Youngdog, fearless prosecutor of evil corporations.

In the lavish corporate restroom, Edwin Puppy slicked down his curly black hair, combed it back, and donned his flamboyant new suit jacket. It was red. Shirt, pants, belt, and shoes could be shared between his two characters. He added a gold watch of alarming proportions. Thus, the modest, self-effacing Mr. Puppy became, with minimal trouble, the flamboyant and theatrical terror of the courtroom.

He added a pair of tortoise shell glasses which should have made him look older but didn't—they just made him look adorable—and an elegant Panama hat for outdoor wear. He already had a trench coat. These items could be stored in his briefcase and closet, ready for use at a moment's notice. The next step was to apply for a prosecutor's job.

The future terror of the courtroom stepped confidently into the elevator of New Courthouse Tower and pushed the button for the 25th floor where the County Attorney's Office reigned in legalistic splendor.[28] Alone in the elevator, he dropped his facade of confidence for a moment, becoming the shy young lawyer once again. The elevator stopped, the bell rang, and Edward Youngdog took a deep breath, altered his stance and affect, and stepped out with his habitual bravado.

"Edward Youngdog, here to see County Attorney Abercrombie," he told the receptionist, leaning confidently on the lovely white birchwood counter in front of her—miles of it, to his inexperienced eye. It went well with the champaign-colored carpet. He momentarily hoped that his paws were not muddy, then shook himself at the silly idea. His human form, one of them, was firmly in place.

"Have a seat, sir, I'll tell him you're here," she said kindly, leaning toward the intercom.

Inner calm, thought Puppy irrelevantly. He certainly didn't want to appear nervous. And there was really no need for her to use that maternal tone—she only looked about twenty-five.

---

28 Yes, we know that's not what legalistic means, but humor us. It sounds so nice there.

D. A. Abercrombie burst from his office like a cheerful explosion. "Youngdog, good to see you!" said the D.A., pumping Puppy's hand. "And right on time, too. Let's see if you'd fit into our office." Puppy found this comment surprising, as he was not that large.

The D.A. wouldn't normally have given so much away on a first meeting, but he was desperate for new assistant D.A.s. They had taken such a drubbing from Horse, Fish, Panther & Puppy in recent days, spread all over the newspaper of course, that several prosecutors had left without notice, and one was even rumored to have jumped out a window.

Gesturing expansively with his arm, he indicated the brass-studded leather chair opposite his desk and assumed his own position behind it. The visitor's chair was a little lower than D.A. Abercrombie's, an old trick for asserting status that Youngdog recognized.

"Well, I'll cut to the chase," said Abercrombie. His visitor instinctively raised his aristocratically pointed nose in anticipation, then took hold of himself; this was not about *birds*, this was about clients. Or suits or something.

The D.A. hadn't noticed the movement consciously, yet perhaps it triggered something in his subconscious mind, because he began, "I suppose you've heard about the Hammersmith case, haven't you?" Youngdog nodded.

"That miserable uptown firm really wiped the floor with us," he continued. "Rather funny your name being Youngdog. Their junior partner is named Puppy. Funny coincidence. Maybe you'll be a match for him, because that boy is keen as mustard. He gave us a lot of trouble."

(Puppy had no memory of this, nor do we, the authors Redborne, Vargas, and Sage. Perhaps the case was heard in some parallel timeline.)

Puppy laughed hollowly. "I believe I've met him, sir, and he's not so tough. Besides I know how he thinks." It was nice to tell the truth for once. Puppy was not used to dissembling and it put a strain on him.

The D.A. abruptly made up his mind. "Well, your forms seem to be in order, your recommendations are impressive, and we need somebody STAT. You're hired! And your first job will be to confront Puppy in the courtroom. I really think you're up to it."

Attorney Youngdog responded not a word, surprising his new employer, who had expected excited gratitude.

Oh well, you never know with these kids, he thought.

THE END

historic steno machine and applied the necessary adhesive, sealing the crack and preventing a tidal wave.

CLERK: Your Honor?
JUDGE: Yes? What *now?*
CLERK: There's one more thing that should perhaps be addressed before we continue with the docket.
JUDGE: Yes?
CLERK: Well, on Planet Earth—
JUDGE: What? More trouble from Earth?
CLERK: Yes, regrettably Your Honor. Several countries within a beautiful continent called Africa are suffering from hunger, war, and a legacy of colonial and local corruption. I believe this needs to be addressed immediately.

The Adequately Magnificent Presence gave a sigh.

JUDGE: Yes, yes, we must address that as well. Of course we must! But I'm afraid I need a quick break.

And this shows that even the highest of manifested beings do get tired and cannot take care of everything all in one day.

His return to the issue came long after everyone in the courtroom had moved on to higher levels of existence (i.e., died), but was only a microsecond later for the victims of the terrible fates he was trying to alleviate. Because, justice delayed is justice denied.

CHAPTER TWENTY-THREE

IF YOU EXPECT SOMETHING SCARY

IT MIGHT ACTUALLY HAPPEN

Back in the old days before everything got really weird, Halycon Sage and/or Karima Vargas Bushnell had written:

Have you ever tried to navigate the post-modern world on a horse? Halycon Sage was fairly sure horses weren't allowed on the freeway, so he kept to the smaller roads. Some places had ordinances about horses on the public streets, but he'd found a way of dealing with this, though he wasn't too proud of himself about it.

When he came into the sort of town a Black friend of his youth had described, running changes on an old commercial, as "the red-

neckiest," he simply pulled out what was in his right saddlebag and put it on his head.

It was a full-out, not too cheap fake Indian headdress obtained on sale from a movie studio. Wearing this regalia, Halycon Sage assumed an earnest and proud expression, rode through the town with head held high, and no one ever bothered him. Little kids cheered or laughed and policemen saluted. They assumed, naturally, that he was the advance guard or tail end of some parade or event they hadn't heard about.

Halycon Sage hoped he never ran into any real Native Americans while he was wearing this getup, because they would have beaten him to a pulp—or worse, laughed till they fell over. Halycon Sage, being possibly of mixed heritage, had a lot of anxiety about whether or not he was a Real Indian. But in spite of his embarrassment, he definitely had to get his horse past the cops, and this worked.

And now here was Sage, minding his own business, walking down a dirt road outside of Dry Creek Gulch when suddenly everything changed. Suddenly he was riding No-Name Stupid—he was very glad to see Stupid as they'd been drifting apart lately—and there were four real, honest-to-God traditional Native Americans riding toward him.

This seemed just fine until he noticed with horror that he was wearing his Fake Indian Chief Getup, just as described in the previous writing.

When they came within speaking distance, Sage opened his mouth and said the first thing that came into his mind.

"How."

Oh, God, no, no, no. He really *had* watched too many old westerns on TV! The word was a real term of greeting from the Lakota tribe, probably better spelled Háu, but it had become the quintessential jerks-making-fun-of-Indians cliché.

Before Sage's earnest desire to sink into the ground precipitated that very occurrence, the apparent leader of the group road forward a few paces and spoke with stone-faced gravity.

"*I know* how. I belong to the Willing Pilgrim's Association," he said, quoting Curly of the Three Stooges. There was a silence; then all five of them cracked up laughing, just as Sage had imagined.

"It's okay, bro, we all do what we have to do," said another man when they were once again able to speak. So that was alright then.

CHAPTER TWENTY-FOUR

CONCERNING TINY BEINGS

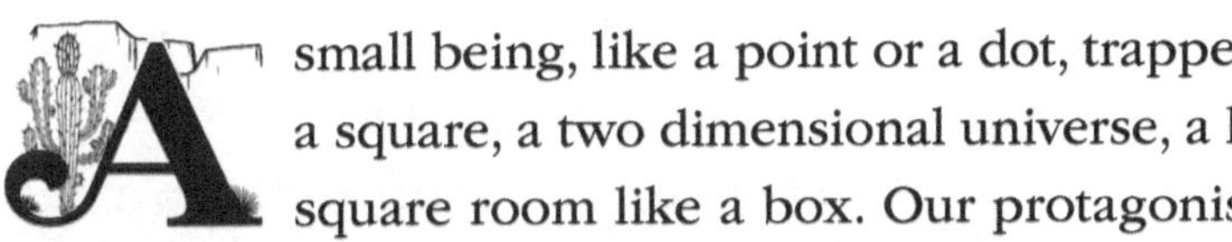 small being, like a point or a dot, trapped in a square, a two dimensional universe, a little square room like a box. Our protagonist of the moment is a dot trapped at the bottom of it trying to get out … Round and round the tiny creature goes, left wall, right wall, front wall, back wall, again and again, trying all these avenues that don't work because it knows nothing else, can conceive nothing else, can imagine nothing else.

Its desperation increases, its speed increases, round and round and round and round, again and again and again and again. It is almost a madness.

Suddenly, a gift from God, the solution presents itself, a new direction previously undreamed of.

The way out is *up!* It had never considered *up* before! The being leaps into the previously unimaginable. The top of the box is open. The being is free.

⌘

There's a quote from C.S. Lewis we can't find right now, something like, "It is for fear of this that prayers remain shallow." And *this,* among other things, is the complete cessation of thoughts and words.

Karima has known this fact for years, for decades. When she was 23, in conversation with her teacher, Swami Atmanishtananda Saraswati of Spokane, Washington (a.k.a. Ruth Reynolds), she had first verbalized it, but she had known it long before that, at least semi-consciously.

The concept of a mantra was new to her; this was 1976 and not everybody knew this stuff. Ruth explained the concept and said, "I'm going to give you some words to repeat."

Karima exploded with rejection. "No!" she said. "No more words! I'm trying to get *rid* of the words!"

Because the ongoing monologue in her head, which for many years had been so entertaining and interesting, had apparently run out of anything worthwhile to say but still would not *shut up!* It was driving her crazy.

Even at 21, even in Seattle, pushing a stroller up a steep hill with a load of laundry and her little daughter, she'd known the way out: to stop the words. Behind the pointless, infinitely repetitive, infinitely boring words, lay Truth. She *knew* it, but she couldn't *do* it. It was a sacrifice like suicide, but unlike suicide, positive.

Over the ensuing years, the words had been good to her. The interest, the insight, the delightful razor of fine-tuned analysis, had returned. The hilarious connections between seemingly unconnected things had also returned.

But now at the possibly final, actual, really-for-sure end of the world, there was no other choice but to take this apparently self-destroying road, this radical, sudden step which had always been available, but never truly desired.

She had to drop all the thoughts, all the words, open and turn still and go *up!* Or maybe just wait. Because if she does that, the cycle of The Sage Chronicles, which she and Halycon Sage are writing together, can be completed, as it could not in any other way.

Now let us tell you about Ahmed the Bug.

Karima was an inveterate rescuer of all beings whenever possible; not necessarily *good* at it, slow and ham-handed at times, but willing.

One sunny day a creature appeared in her house: moving, alive with the mysterious life that animates all living things, but tiny as a pencil dot, smaller than the head of a pin. She wanted to scoop him up on a piece of typing paper and take him out, release him into the glorious morning, into the sunshine, to live his little life. But some tiny, clumsy motion as she was transferring him onto the paper, or moving the paper—she forgets now—and he was dead. The little dot had stopped moving. It looked just the same really, a tiny black speck, but there was all the difference in the world, like the difference between a beautiful living woman and the identical woman laid out on an undertaker's table, coiffed and made up, but still a corpse.

And it was heartbreaking. We know this sounds stupid compared to all that we see in this world, but it was the same tragedy really. That which was alive and moving is so no longer. The only difference was in scale.

So Karima did a silly, odd thing, but the only thing she could see that might be done. Posthumously—she used to think this was pronounced post-humously, like whatever comes after the enriching leaf mold is absorbed into the soil, bringing new nutrients, bringing new life, and may it happen to this Earth—posthumously, she gave him *bayat*.

She gave him initiation into her Sufi order. She said the simplest form of the holy words and it felt right and real. It took only a minute or two. He was a tiny, tiny bug and didn't need an elaborate ceremony.

Part of this ceremony, a part which happens at the end, is the giving of a new name. And lo, his name was Ahmed the Bug.

When she told this to her Shaykha, her teacher for the 30 years since the one who first enlightened her had passed, the teacher laughed and accepted it. This was a woman who sometimes didn't understand small things but who, with Karima at least, always understood the big ones. She laughed and accepted it. So now, across time and space, across dimensions, across from "life" to "death," we salute and greet Ahmed the Bug. *As salaamu aleykum wa rahmatullah wa barakatu huuuuuuuuuuuu.*

And the point of all this is that if the Tesseract, the unimaginable super-cube, is to be completed, the authors must do what Ahmed the Bug did, and what A. Square did in *Flatland*.

They must drop everything they know, and go *UP!* Oddly, in matters of this kind, higher and deeper amount to the same thing, leaving each individual free to conceive this journey in whichever way feels most comfortable.

It's like fishing. The person on the bank can't create the fish. You must be very, very still, alert and open, and wait for them to come.

CHAPTER TWENTY-FIVE

IN THE COURT OF THE MULTIVERSE

Chaos erupted all up and down the courthouse hall, so loud it exploded through the soundproofed doors in a cacophony of trans-galactic languages, human, animal, and alien noises, and inchoate howls of pure outrage and fury. It sounded like the End Times in stereo.

It sounded like the Bug Butter scene from *A Civil Campaign* by Lois McMaster Bujold, or the scene from Michael Moorcock's *Dancers at the End of Time* where club-bearing Victorian policemen chase the consummately rude alien Lat in circles while mad inventor Branart Morphail spins around the ceiling in his defective time machine. It sounded like all that and worse.

This was how it began.

⅋

As far as anybody knew, it was an ordinary day on the third floor of the Intergalactic Time-Loose Actual Justice for All Beings Court House. It was called the third floor out of sentiment for historical writings and for convenience; it was actually Floor 3279143812B, or something like that, not precisely locatable in time or space unless you knew just where to go.

One of the first tests of a new young lawyer appearing before the Interdimensional Intergalactic Transtemporal Bar was *finding* the place. A lot of them ended up at the Interdimensional Intergalactic Transtemporal Bar on One-Million Twenty-Seventh Street and Fifty-First Avenue drinking Pan-Galactic Gargle Blasters[29] and losing their cases to summary judgement for non-appearance.

Many of these attorneys were still roaming the various outer planets of the known or unknown Multiverse trying to avoid their vengeful clients. Since all frontiers have certain things in common no matter how far-flung they are, an Old West atmosphere prevailed in these outer reaches. The places looked like scenes out of *Firefly*, *Serenity*, or *Defiance*.

---

29 Described in Douglas Adams' *Hitchhiker's Guide to the Galaxy* as "the best drink in existence," which feels like "having your brains smashed out by a slice of lemon wrapped round a large gold brick."

EDITORS' NOTE: The Sci-Fi *Defiance*, not the military one. If you have not seen these, do so immediately. Your life may depend on it! It probably won't, but if you don't, you'll miss meeting some really cool alien races, not to mention, in *Defiance*, one of the best character arcs ever written. Do not skip episodes or you will miss the point.

We will introduce you to the courtroom gently with what should be a relatively normal, everyday case. You may notice that some of the attorneys are already known to you.

Old Rumblethunder[30] was presiding. It is a peculiarity of the intergalactic and multidimensional judicial system that even the highest authorities often hear the most ordinary cases. No one in the known Multiverse outranked Old Rumblethunder, but like all the other judges and justices, he took his turn in the intergalactic equivalent of traffic court.

His enormous tank had been polished till it sparkled, and the water inside it cascaded around in luminescent green-blue waves made possible by the few feet of 'air' at the top of the tank. It was a majestic sight to behold.

This justice was so old and honored that everyone had forgotten his name, but he has been mentioned

---

30 Even in the deepest deeps and highest heights of the Multiverse you cannot entirely squelch brash young attorneys. But they stood in awe of him really, and the secret affection in which they held him was based on his unchallenged reputation for fairness and impartiality.

earlier in this narrative as the Adequately Magnificent Presence and also appears in the preface to *The Way Beyond* where he is referred to as The Eminence. We will call him simply the Judge.

JUDGE: Next case.

And here there was an interruption. Of course there was!

CHAPTER TWENTY-SIX

A MATTER OF GREAT CONCERN

CLERK: Your Honor, an urgent matter has come to our attention. It must be addressed immediately!

JUDGE: Can't this wait?

CLERK: I'm sorry, Your Honor, but no, it can't! We need an immediate ruling. It has been discovered that, in many places throughout time, space, and the Multiverse, *innocent beings are serving time for crimes they did not commit! Or crimes they committed, but which, due to circumstances, were not actually their fault!*

JUDGE: *What?* Am I *hearing you* correctly?

His particular species was not susceptible to deafness, but this news seemed unbelievable.

CLERK: Yes, Honor, I'm afraid it's true. We have it on the best authority!

If you live on the physically manifested planets, you probably think *everyone* should know this, but sometimes at the highest levels, details which affect those in less exalted positions can be entirely missed.

JUDGE: Well, *let them out! Immediately!*

CLERK: Yes, Your Honor.

JUDGE: And arrange adequate redress and compensation in line with what they have suffered unjustly. Tropical islands with their best friends, true love, study at the most prestigious universities, big parties, delicious food and drink if they are material creatures. What is the expression? "Whatever floats their boat?"

CLERK: I believe that is the expression, Your Honor.

JUDGE: So ordered, then. See to it. Oh, and any time they have served unjustly is to be refunded, with appropriate compensation. Do I make myself clear?

CLERK: Yes, Your Honor.

The Adequately Magnificent Presence made a quick scan of the Multiverse, being suddenly drawn to a small, bright place that seemed to have a lot of problems.

"What's this Gaza business?" he asked.

"*Oh*," said the clerk and the court reporter together, also the bailiff. Being lower in the chain of being than the Presence, they could sometimes see the details of these tiny places more clearly. Because they were nearer.

"*Oh, that*," said the clerk, the court reporter, and the bailiff.

There was a silence while they delivered the information telepathically to the Judge.

JUDGE: We'll recess for half a micro-unit.

Alone in his chambers, which was located in the back of his enormous tank and protected by a privacy screen, the Adequately Magnificent Presence Justice Rumblethunder broke down in great heaving sobs. Never before in his billions of years of existence had he done such a thing. After a little while, a timeless time, he collected himself and returned to his bench. But the more observant of those present in the court room noticed that the water level in his tank was higher than before.

JUDGE: Next case.

At this point His Honor banged his gavel with such force as to crack the tank, and water began leaking out. (Please don't ask what he banged it *on*, as the level of detail required to address some of these issues is becoming annoying.) His court reporter, no stranger to this particular emergency, leaped from behind her

"We certainly must address all this," repeated the Judge when he returned, "These clowns on Earth are supposed to have free will, but let's see what we can do within those parameters."

He had not forgotten anything. He never did.

The following note has just been delivered to us by a passing Mad Grammarian, and it might as well go here as anywhere as we seem to have a bit of blank space.

NOTE FROM A MAD GRAMMARIAN: During Karima's, or Sage's, or possibly both their childhoods, the matter of the Oxford Comma* was confusing. Because every year, whoever was teaching Reading or English or whatever it was called reversed the policy that was taught the year before. So, while they have generally acquiesced to using the darned thing, they are unwilling to follow the hidebound rule that, within any text, they must always do one thing or the other, either use it or leave it out. Because there are times when it is nice, pleasant, and appropriate and other times when it is *not!* So, should you, the reader, in your own etymological wisdom** find a place where one is left out, it was *done on purpose!*

And while we're on the subject of consistency, remember the maxim that, "A foolish consistency is the hobgoblin of small minds." So it's barely possible that throughout this text, you will find the title of *Puppy for the Defense* rendered either with or without a comma after "Or" in the second phrase of the title: "Or, the Prosecution ..." Thank you for your attention

---

* You know, that comma that goes before the last "and" in a series. Because some teachers taught that the "and" *replaced* the comma, while others taught that both were necessary.

** Not *ento*mological, because that means *bugs!*

CHAPTER TWENTY-SEVEN

AN UNEXPECTED SETBACK

**Puppy for the Defense!
Or, the Prosecution …**

Chapter Six

So it was that Edwin Puppy, wearing his new disguise, found himself approaching the many courtrooms on the third floor of Courts Tower. The doors all looked alike except that the numbers on them were different. Puppy was a bit nervous, but Edward Youngdog knew he *had* this! He was nothing if not self-confident. This was his first case as a prosecutor! How exciting.

The room was 302. Or 203. Or maybe 303. He stood for a moment indecisively outside the door of Courtroom 304, then swung it open and walked in with a firm and confident step, bypassing the defense table to take his place as a prosecutor. A couple of other prosecuting attorneys were there and welcomed him casually. He slid into his seat, grateful to have arrived and be situated.

"All rise," said the court clerk, and the judge entered, majestic in his black robe. The attorneys, court reporter, and assorted spectators rose to their feet, then sat back down at a casual wave from the judge.

"Davis vs. Rattlesnake Mining, Inc.," called the clerk. And right there, Lawyer Youngdog should have known he was in trouble, because he'd taken employment with the county *prosecutor's office,* an arm of the *government*, not with a plaintiff's firm that represented private individuals or brought class action suits. If he were appearing in a case that matched his new job title, the entity he spoke for would have been the county, not a class representative!

Part of the confusion arose from the fact that there happened to be *three* cases involving coal companies taking place that day, two civil and one criminal, in rooms 302, 203, and 304, but that barely scratched the surface of the problem.

It has often been stated that two wrongs don't make a right, but Gabriel Redborne and the writers of this Chronicle have all observed that such is not the case— two wrongs *frequently* make a right! And it appeared that this was just such a situation.

Puppy, instead of joining a civil firm that represented plaintiffs, had inadvertently joined the County Attorney's

Office, whose job it was to prosecute criminals. That was his first mistake.

His whole goal in perpetrating this elaborate hoax had been to defend the righteous cause of Class Representative Davis and the injured mineworkers against the big, oppressive coal company. And in this situation, defending an injured party pretty much meant prosecuting a bad actor, a seeming reversal which still had Puppy scratching his head.[31]

However, his second mistake appeared to have canceled out his first! He had not only taken the wrong job, he had come to the wrong courtroom! And just as with his momentary head-scratch, nobody seemed to have noticed.

He only had to remember to say "Plaintiff" and "Defendant" instead of "County" and "Accused." He was actually in the *right* court room, indeed, at the very table of those whose job it was to go after the coal company!

Early in his law school career, the difference between civil and criminal procedure had been carefully explained to Mr. Puppy. Unfortunately, he'd been asleep at the time, sitting far back in the enormous lecture room, arms folded and chin resting on his chest, a look of utmost concentration on his sleeping face. As the professor was explaining that in a *criminal* case, a government entity

---

31 He briefly scratched his head with his right hind foot, moving it in a pleasing circular motion, then dropped it in horror, resuming his lawyerly form. And something funny was going on here, because nobody appeared to have noticed. But he did catch an odd little smile on the face of one of the defending attorneys.

charges a defendant while in a *civil* case one individual or entity sues another, Mr. Puppy gave forth a gentle snore.

Only those nearest him noticed, and after he awoke, the fact that in both kinds of procedure one side was sometimes referred to as "the Defendant" made him erroneously believe that he knew what was going on.

The young law student had good reason to be tired. Unable to decide between his longed-for dream of becoming a lawyer and an equally passionate dedication to animal rescue, he was lately finding his legal studies compromised to the point of threatening his graduation. He had been up all night delivering a large litter of kittens. Mother and kittens were doing well.

And abruptly he shook off all these thoughts of the past and stood up as a practicing attorney for the very first time. It was a moment of glory.

"Who speaks for the state?" asked the judge.

"I do, Your Honor," said Edward Youngdog.

State, plaintiff, he thought to himself. *Potato, potahto.*

CHAPTER TWENTY-EIGHT

EDWIN PUPPY IN DRY CREEK GULCH

Edwin Puppy unlocked the door and went into the little warren of a law office, which appeared to be unoccupied, though it was already 7:30 a.m. He looked around the front room with pleasure, enjoying the slightly beat-up wooden furniture, sun washed by the strong Nevada light. This was his domain, the place from which he could finally fight for justice, unhampered by the silly rules of the Alternate Universe.

According to the fascinated Squidish observers, Puppy was anomalous in two ways, fully as unique as Halycon Sage himself. First, he was one of the very few who had stepped out of some writer's mind and assumed a real identity, complete with consciousness and free will. But several others had done this, including Tarzun and the Apocalypse Zombie, so it was not unprecedented.

His true uniqueness lay in what he had *done* with his situation. He was the only person, as far as anyone knew, who had intentionally moved, lock, stock and barrel, into Dry Creek Gulch out of somebody's novel, which had apparently been set in the Alternate Universe, what had been 'the world' before Preisczech, Sage, and the Squidren had split everything in two.

Puppy had come in wanting to work on his big coal mining case, but somehow the sunlight on the floating dust motes was calling him outside. *I'll take a stroll around the new shops*, he thought. There seemed to be one of these springing up every day, like mushrooms. In fact, there was even one that *looked* like a mushroom. He took his hat from the brass hat rack and headed out the door.

The first place to the right was an old-fashioned candy store, its windows displaying different flavors of fudge and brightly colored taffy and loops of red and black licorice. While he sometimes had a sweet tooth, right now Puppy wasn't in the mood. He wanted to investigate some of the stranger stores he'd noticed.

Leather Works, a shoe and saddle repair shop, attractive but normal. Nice boots. The House of Cats looked a bit weird, but he'd check that out some other time.

Crazy Melvin's Monster Radio Store. Sure, why not? He walked up to the big metal doors, grabbed an industrial-looking handle, pulled it hard, and stepped inside.

"RWAAAAAWRRRRR!" came a grating, deafening voice.

Something huge and green rushed at him from the back of the store, wanting either to welcome him or to eat him, he wasn't sure which. The thing was enormous, 20 or 30 feet high, and he didn't have time to guess its weight right now.

"MAY I HELP YOU?" came the grating, grinding voice. There was a definite saurian look to this character, a tyrannosaurus or allosaurus, but it was not entirely real looking, more like a blow-up monster from some fairground attraction or extravagant Christmas display. It opened its mouth. Its teeth were enormous, maybe six inches long for the protruding incisors that extended over its lips.

"WELL??? WHAT CAN I DO FOR YOU??" the thing roared, beginning to sound impatient. With both its tiny, claw-ended arms, it held something out to him. Puppy took his courage in both hands, or paws—in this moment of stress and confusion, he was not quite sure about his *own* physical form. Everything was just too new. He stepped forward to see what the thing was holding. Vastly small and ordinary in contrast to the creature presenting it, it was a small ... black ... plastic ... entirely ordinary ... AM/FM ... radio.

Puppy turned and fled.

CHAPTER TWENTY-NINE

"EVERYBODY WHO'S ANYBODY"

A flier was blowing down the main street of Dry Creek Gulch, which right now was living up to its name. The river was alright, but the little subsidiary creeks were bone dry. A tumble weed rolled by, followed by another and another.

Caught in the branches of the second or third tumbleweed was *another* flier. The Squid reached out a tentacle and examined it, drawing it close to his ruby-red eye.

It read,

Everybody who is anybody will be there!
The First Post-Modernist Minimalist Neo-Symbolist
Pseudo-Realist
Literary Conference of Dry Creek Gulch.

The Squid found this puzzling. "Everybody who is anybody ..." But everybody was somebody, weren't they? Because if they weren't, then they would be nobody and there would be no point in talking about them because they would not exist.

Perhaps this was referring to the imaginary characters that populated the books?

The Squid shook his heads. (His grandmother had been part Chillidian and he took after her in some ways. The rest of the Squidren politely ignored the second head, which accorded with their notion of good manners but which made the head very bitter when it had something to say!)

That explanation did not make sense because, in the first place, a number of the characters who started out as fictional had *turned* real, and even disallowing that possibility, they had different and even complex characteristics just like those with more than two dimensions, didn't they? So how were they not people?

Thus the problem remained. And the only conclusion the Squid could draw was that, "Everyone who is anyone will be there," meant that *everyone* would be there! How would the organizers fit them all in? Even if they abandoned the town library and held the conference in the old hotel, which would need some furbishing up, there would not be room! Would there be room for them all in the big communal log cabin or the giant circus tent that was sometimes set up outside of Dry Creek Gulch?

Emphatically not! (*Lymphaticly not! haha* thought the Squid, who like all his kind was word obsessed and also fond of puns, even stupid, pointless ones.)

Never mind that, chimed in a telepathic friend. (*A Squid? The horse No-Name Stupid? You couldn't always tell who was speaking.) How wide is this "everybody" designation?*

The town? The state? The galaxy? The Multiverse???

The Squid had a final thought on the matter. *If everybody who's anybody will be there, I will be there too! But there's no need to be shy, because nobody will notice me among the huge crowd of every single being in the Multiverse.*

So his personal shyness problem was solved, but like a dog with a bone, the Squid could not quite abandon the issue. There were a lot of beings in the Multiverse! The only conceivable way to fit them all in was to just print their names and let them tune in that way. Or maybe even *recite* the names, which would take far more time, but even less room.

Not taking Earth preferences into account, the Squid did not see any problem with this solution. The Squidren could often take two or three weeks for just an ordinary quick-break conversation at the water cooler.[32]

---

32 Yes, alright, don't be so pedantic. *Of course* we mean the Squid equivalent of a water cooler, a place where colleagues gather for a quick break. Maybe the SquidPool.

CHAPTER THIRTY

A MINOR ANNOYANCE

Preisczech snickered. "I think you have some competition." — Sage's Multiverse Mini-Series.

Suddenly, the persistent and nondescript young man who'd approached Sage before about some annoying conference was once again at his side. It was getting so you couldn't walk down the street in Dry Creek Gulch anymore.

"It's about the First Annual Post-Modernist Minimalist Neo-Symbolist Pseudo-Realist School of Literature Conference of Dry Creek Gulch," said the man importantly.

So, it had a name now.

"You remember, we talked about it before," he added encouragingly.

Sage had been hoping there'd be some catastrophe so that it would be cancelled, but he was evidently out of luck and the thing was proceeding as planned.

Since basic survival issues had mostly been solved, the townspeople were focusing on the ornaments of life: leisure, sports, the arts. Which would have been fine, even a writers' convention would have been okay, but this one was specifically focused on the school of literature that he himself had pioneered before the Event.

Sage had two problems with this. For one thing, he was shy and had never liked being the center of attention. He hadn't minded it so much when he'd been teaching or lecturing about something that interested him, but the focus of *this* regrettable gathering, at least while he was speaking, would be himself and his books. It would be *me, me, me*, and he hated that.

Additionally, while the other writers involved—his copycats—wrote two- or three-sentence novels that superficially resembled his own, their work was mostly drivel: shallow and derivative, obvious and attention-seeking, and far more geared to building their reputations as authors than to actually saying anything.

No matter how silly Sage's own work might look from the outside, beneath each tiny mini-novel were depths and implications, the stuff that Ruby had been able to get lost in for hours in the old days before she met him. And just to be polite, he would have to pretend that all or most of the other stuff was *good.*

Okay, a few of the ones he'd seen were not too bad, maybe something interesting would turn up, or maybe he could help them improve their craft. It wasn't like he had anything *else* to do.

Sage felt a stab of self-pity and sternly suppressed it. He was momentarily considering Ruby. She was gone for good, might as well admit it.

"Of course, there's one more person we'll need to make the event a success. Besides yourself, I mean," continued the man, breaking in on his thoughts. "The only other really great writer in town. The only one besides yourself who had an international reputation before The Event."

This guy—Mr. Brown was his name, Sage suddenly remembered—had apparently been talking for a while now, but Sage, letting his mind wander, had not been listening. Maybe it mattered.

"I know there's been some tension between the two of you in the past, but his presence here really *is* essential. Of course Basel Vasselschnauzer is just as famous as the two of *you*, but he's a *critic*, not a writer. So though he'll be participating, it won't be in the same way. And Sophie McGregor, though she's also brilliant, is young and untested. And then the other writers are virtually unknown, through no fault of their own, of course. There's no lack of great talent, I mean."

He stopped nervously. Sage was mildly amused. Did this dude think Sage was a passionate advocate of all these copycats and hangers-on, considering them his protégés? Suddenly Sage felt a bit guilty. Perhaps that was how he *should* feel. He resolved to be better in the future.

Mr. Brown was still babbling on.

"Of course his works are not *short*; we'll have to widen the conference title beyond "mini-novels" since his briefest work is around a thousand pages. And his books aren't very *cheerful* either. They lack the warmth, brevity, and subtle humor that characterize your *own* brilliant work ..."

If he went on like this much longer, Sage was going to throw up. He did not like flattery and was not a big fan of this guy.

"But as I say, leaving him out would be unthinkable," the fellow droned on. "I know he has sometimes been called depressing, life-denying, a nihilist, but he's an undoubted intellectual ..."

Suddenly Sage knew, with cold horror creeping up the back of his neck, who Mr. Brown was talking about.

It was the author of *The Black Gray Dark; I'm Fabulous, You're a Necrotic Collection of Worm Food; Decay; The Swamp of Despair; Nothing*, and other such travesties. The man who had kidnapped Ruby and Basel Vasselschnauzer and caused the loss of Preisczech's Nanobot-controlling whistle. His would-be nemesis who had fancied himself a supervillain, redeemed at least briefly during the Great Awakening described at the end of Sage's second long novel *The Book of Squidly Light*.

But who knew what the guy was getting up to now, whether his transformation had stuck or whether he'd reverted to his former ways? Sometimes people backslid. Who knew what he was like by now?

(The uncanny way his thoughts echoed almost word-for-word the thoughts of Ruby on the same subject provided some evidence that, despite their various misunderstandings, they really *did* belong together.)

This man had not been seen in Dry Creek Gulch for many months, and Sage had been content to let the matter rest, hoping he was firmly relegated to the past.

Mr. Brown was talking about the nihilist author who had twice tried to destroy the world. Archvillain Niemand Kompt.

When he heard about this, Basel Vasselschnauzer was going to have kittens.

CHAPTER THIRTY-ONE

THE SCIENCE OR
THE PUPPY?

If Dry Creek Gulch had still followed any normal rules of science, physics and whatnot, after being tinkered with by Preisczech, the Squidren, and the Nanobots, they were gone by now. I believe we have already explained this.

UNIDENTIFIED VOICE: No, you haven't! And we're going to need some answers!

SECOND VOICE: You really need to explain some of these threads. The science in this series has always been ridiculous, but you got away with it because people were diverted by other things. But now it's gone completely off the rails. You'll have to pull yourselves together.

FIRST VOICE: And what's with this Edwin Puppy character? That's just his *name*, right? But what do you mean by *"his hands (or paws)"* and *"Everything was just too new?"* He's not really a *puppy*, is he?

SECOND VOICE: Right. You explained, actually quite elegantly, about his move from a mini-novel to the real world of Dry Creek Gulch and his motivations, or at least you foreshadowed what was happening in an interesting way, but what about this other stuff? Quit stalling. Is he *a man or a puppy?*

FIRST VOICE: And which of these incongruities are you going to deal with first? You'd better do it fast before something *else* impossible happens!

SECOND VOICE: Obviously the science is much more important than the puppy thing, which is surely a mere bagatelle.

FIRST VOICE (Smirking, if a voice can smirk): *Bagatelle?* Does anyone *say* that anymore? Will anyone even know what it means? Of course they won't!

SECOND VOICE: It's a perfectly good word. Just because *you're* uneducated—

FIRST VOICE: Do Sage and Karima even know what it means?

SECOND VOICE: I wouldn't bet on it. They're just like Basel Vasselschnauzer: They never look anything up.

THIRD VOICE: Do you froods[33] mind if we continue with the chapter? Sage and Preisczech are having a discussion somewhen on the issue of accurate science; we can check in on that. And we can show you a chapter or two

---

33 From Douglas Adams' *Hitchhiker's Guide to the Galaxy*, a really amazingly together person.

of *Puppy for the Defense!* to explain the other matter. Which do you want first?

SECOND VOICE: The science!

FIRST VOICE: The puppy!

THIRD VOICE (In a tone of exaggerated patience): Okay, I'll flip a coin.

CHAPTER THIRTY-TWO

THE SCIENCE

"Your science is the problem," said Preisczech bluntly. "Or rather your lack of it." His English had taken a quantum leap, achieving a certain elegance, though he still retained his charming accent. Sprung sentences had become few and far between, occurring only when he became excited. But he was excited now.

"I mean, what is this with *match?*" He thumbed quickly through the rumpled pages of *The Way Beyond*, Sage's autobiography lightly disguised as fiction. "See, page 43, you and I are talking. And I say I invent a thing to stop explosions, stops bombs exploding, and you say what about other stuff that won't work like internal combustion engine and I say so what, who cares and you say, *you* say (reading), 'But what about electricity? None of the coal-fired plants would work, would they?

Natural gas-powered stuff wouldn't work. *You couldn't even strike a match!'"*

He held up a match triumphantly: Exhibit A! He had brought it with him. (And no, it didn't work.)

"That has always been the problem with your world building, my friend," concluded Preisczech shaking his head sadly. "You abrogate the basic laws of science."

"I wasn't *interested* in science," said Sage defensively. He was aware of this weakness but had brushed it from his consciousness, having too many other things to worry about.

"Well, you'd better get interested now," concluded his friend. "Because the manure is about to hit the propeller." Preisczech still needed a little work on his English idioms.

Perhaps this was why everything in Dry Creek Gulch was increasingly wonky. It was an open secret now that Sage had recreated everything there with his mind, saving this one small area, fortunately split off by the Nanobots, from the mechanical, thoughtless, and self-seeking cruelty that was overtaking portions of the Alternate Universe.

But there were problems. Water didn't flow uphill very often, but it had happened, along with other silly inconsistencies, and you can't really live that way. You can't plan.

Halycon Sage was stuck. In the years building up to the final apotheosis, he had thrown everything he had at the problem of saving the world, studying and researching, and had applied all the things he enjoyed and was good at: empathy, imagination, conversation, creative writing, world religions, prayers and ceremonies, communicating across cultures, history, and foreign languages.

He did not like science beyond a dab of anthropology and sociology and so had ignored it. But if science can be loosely defined as objectivity and observation, then mystics across time, place, and religion have observed certain patterns affecting world views, civilizations, and human beings. The first two rise and peak and fall as regularly and predictably as ocean waves. But a human, any sentient being, is something different.

Sage had observed that in life you eventually revisit each situation you've already visited, but higher and higher up, as in Karen Armstrong's book *The Spiral Staircase*. Again and again and again. Sage had actually come to this realization on his own, as a child or a young teen, and had found it confirmed by the words of the Knowers. So here he was again.

He sighed, accepting the inevitable. He'd already written it in his original autobiography. *For this, a scientific solution was needed. He would have to find Preisczech.*

Since Preisczech was right here, he didn't need to be found, anyway, which was a good thing, as the process of finding each other again had been long and arduous. But somehow his friend understood something that he did not.

State the problem. What has gone wrong with our tiny civilization after the good ending, after everything was solved, conditions in the outside world unknown, but Dry Creek Gulch buttoned up, safe and secure?

Well, holes had started opening up to the rest of the world, like thinning clouds revealing unimagined vistas.

Sage shook his head. "Unimagined vistas" sounded exalted, inspiring, hopeful. The new scenes revealed through the thinning of whatever protection the Squidren had thrown around the village were nothing like that.

A passing Squid remarked, "We've noticed the basic instability of the laws of physics in your particular version of the EarthWorld, Mr. Sage. We thought you liked it like that."

"I did," said Sage, turning back to Preisczech, who had been waiting patiently while he was thinking things through. "But it doesn't work anymore. The rest of the world is coming back."

"Why didn't you tell me the science in my books was such a disaster?" he asked his comrade. "A match won't burn? What?"

Preisczech shrugged. "I didn't want to hurt your feelings, my friend. And you weren't ready to hear it."

Sage had a final thought before they went their separate ways.

"And what's this SUx^2BU? What's that about?"

Preisczech replied, "Ah, that, my friend, is the key to everything."

171

CHAPTER THIRTY-THREE

A PUPPY IN THE HOUSE OF CATS[34]

With an Interruption by Halycon Sage

Remember last time when we left Mr. Edwin Puppy, Esq? He had just fled in terror from the Thing that had emerged from Crazy Melvin's Monster Radio Store. We'll pick it up from there.

Ahem …

Edwin Puppy shook himself violently, like a labrador emerging from the water. That had been a close call!

He proceeded down the block. There was another storefront he was remembering … ah, there it was. The big leaping dolphin sign which read, in colorful neon that *worked*:

---

34 Though the names are similar, we don't really think this title has any connection with Anais Nin's *A Spy in the House of Love*. Of course we can't be sure. Puppy *does* have some of the qualities of a spy.

Cetacean Nation: Come See
What We're Up To!

It wasn't a store yet—maybe that was planned for later. At the moment, it was a small booth, such as could once be seen at pop-up events and street fairs. The *smaller* sign directly over the booth read simply *Cetacean Creations*. Pinned to the walls and laid out on the counter were extravagantly designed clothing and jewelry: leaping dolphins and porpoises, majestic whales, blue waves and foaming whitecaps, all kinds of sea birds. The colors were vibrant: deep-water blue and tropical-bay turquoise, seaweed green, the yellow of sunlight, the red, peach, purple, and magenta of tropical flowers.

As we read earlier, "The empty chair, presumably to be occupied by the proprietress of this small establishment, was oddly shaped. Very oddly."

The occupant of the chair was an enormous sea mammal, and on closer inspection, the whale- or dolphin- or whatever-shaped chair was not actually a chair, but some kind of *tank*. The creature was apparently just finishing a little lecture of the sort given at historical sites, national parks, zoos, and other kinds of displays and presentations. The voice was deep, booming, and musically intricate, but some kind of Squid-like technology was simultaneously translating every word as the creature spoke, creating a beautiful and impressive affect. The small audience listened attentively.

"Thank you for your time. If you've paid attention, you should now be able to distinguish the various types of cetaceans with ease, whether you encounter us in the sea, our natural environment, or on land using our new post-modern technologies. Remember, of all cetaceans, the toothed whales (*odontoceti*, a suborder which includes all whales and dolphins with teeth) most obviously display sexual dimorphism.

"Sexual dimorphism," said Edwin Puppy stepping forward. "Sounds hot."

It was not Puppy's fault. Having only recently assumed his current form, he was insufficiently acculturated, and since his move from the Alternate Universe to Dry Creek Gulch—a second huge and disorienting transition—things were even worse. He was trying to be hip, cool, and unshockable, but that wasn't at all what was called for here and he had no idea how to do it anyway.

Heads turned, faces showing varying degrees of disapproval. The nonhuman face of the speaker wore an expression of disgust, as if she had just stepped on something thrown up by a squid. (Please remember that when first encountering an unfamiliar culture, you should avoid topics that might be seen as inappropriate or controversial.)

Puppy retreated abashed and ran into the yard in front of the *next* place down the road, another establishment he'd been curious about.

There were two things about Edwin Puppy. Well, there were probably more than two, but there were two that concern us at this moment. With the persistence of a dog burying or digging up a bone, he could not leave any matter alone once it had aroused his curiosity. He might have made a good newspaper reporter.

We were going to tell you what the second thing was, but we went off on a tangent and forgot it. Maybe later. The main point is that, having investigated the other stores on Main Street to his satisfaction, he kept wondering what *this* place was and on this particular day, on the run from his embarrassing faux pas at Cetacean Creations, he ran into their yard.

A sign read,

The House of Cats

This name seemed strange. Though he had not been in his present form or forms very long, (as was mentioned earlier), Edwin Puppy was familiar with two similar-sounding but apparently wildly divergent terms, "cat house" and "cat café." He wasn't exactly sure what the words on the sign intended or what the establishment was offering, and he wasn't sure the proprietors were certain either. Puppy felt a bit baffled, caught on the back foot, as it were. Fortunately, he had four of these, at least sometimes, so was not likely to lose his balance, either socially or physically. (The English idiom "caught on the back foot" means being at a disadvantage, surprised, and feeling that one needs to defend oneself.)

We interrupt this chapter
to bring you an important message
from Halycon Sage
— The Editors

Hi guys. Sorry about this.

I'm actually the one responsible for the House of Cats subplot, which was going to be a whole big thing with Edwin Puppy, but after getting two long chapters into it, I found that the more I wrote, the more irritated with it I became, until I decided *Nope!* and deleted the whole thing. This can happen to authors.

You know, like the time I started writing a vampire novel about Ruby and the Dirty Dog Gang and then had the good sense to tear the whole thing up before she saw it. Here's part of it again with a little of what happened afterward in case you've forgotten.

And where and when, Dear Reader, did the denizens of the Dirty Dog sleep, known only to themselves? And why did they spend all day, sweet spring mornings, lazy summer afternoons, and invigorating autumn mid-days, in a dark, dark bar? And why was Ruby's skin so white, and her hair and eyes so black, and her lips so very, very red? And why were her polished fingernails so long? Was it only to frighten possible attackers? And why was Wolf named Wolf, and why were his long, long, hair and grizzled beard so very, very thick? Oh, surely, surely not. Oh surely, this isn't that sort of book! There has been no hint, no foreshadowing at all. Oh, surely not. But yes, Dear Reader, yes—it is that sort of book ...

He put down his pen. He couldn't do this. He couldn't do it to himself, and he couldn't do it to Ruby, sleeping peacefully beside him, her face a dusky gold in the morning light, not white at all. He didn't need to be a horror writer. There was enough horror in the world without him adding any more.

Maybe he really *would* write a book about cows. You saw them often in the west, peaceful cows grazing in the wide green fields, standing still in sun and dappled shade, or moving slowly, gathering together under trees to shelter from the heat, feeling the perfumed wind and occasional rain. Beautiful animals, calm and gentle. Until one day—more horror.

Oh, well, it was a good life while it lasted. Something got us all in the end, cows or humans. Hopefully the end would be quick, or noble, or something. Maybe he'd just go back to writing *Boo Radley Goes Hawaiian*.

The End

CHAPTER THIRTY-FOUR

PREISCZECH EXPLAINS AGAIN

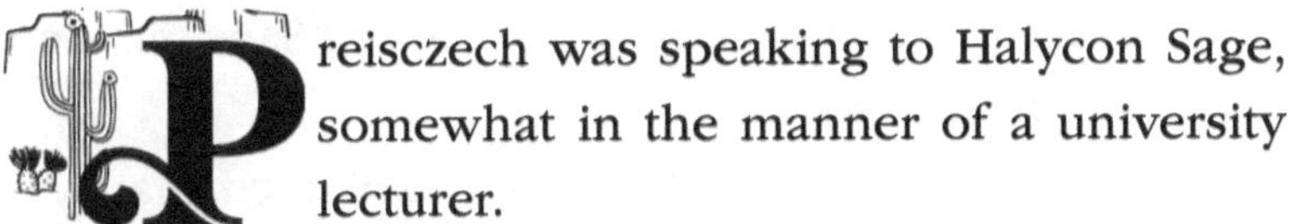

reisczech was speaking to Halycon Sage, somewhat in the manner of a university lecturer.

"So, among the technologies developed between the Event and the current time period in Dry Creek Gulch and the Alternate Universe (which are running concurrent at the moment), only two of them concern us here: SwitchingUp™ and Sux²BU."

"Got it," said Sage, pleased that Preisczech appeared to be in a concise mood and there would be no long, boring science lecture.

"And you know about SwitchingUp™, right? You read the paper I gave you?"

"Check," said Sage.

"And you're being zapped into the future, or the Indeterminate In-Between Space, at any moment now, right? You have no control over it? And it seems to be getting more frequent?"

"Right," said Sage. "Last time it ruined an excellent berry pie I was baking," he added in an aggrieved tone of voice.

"Sage, never mind the pie. Concentrate."

"Check," said Sage again. This was interesting but it was a beautiful day and he wanted to get out *into* it, not be stuck here listening to Preisczech. He didn't even know where "here" was; it was a sort of undefined neutral gray space, because neither of them had bothered to fill in any of the details.

"What does Sux^2BU do, anyway?" asked Sage, making one final effort to focus.

"Oh," said Preisczech. "I haven't explained that yet? I thought I did."

He paused a moment in thought, then closed his eyes and looked down, trying to find the most simple and direct way to describe the momentous effect of his latest invention, the thing that could pull the entire earth plane back from the brink of madness.

"First let me explain how the formula got its name," he began.

Sage sighed. It looked like this might take a while after all.

"Of course the name is the *actual formula*—none of you people have transcribed it right, by the way—but it's also named for the *effect* it has on people. When it first starts working, it is disorienting and extremely uncomfortable, and once it starts, there's no way to stop it till the process is complete. It just has to be endured."

Sage wished he had a watch to look at.

"You see, my friend," the scientist continued, emphasizing the gravity of this moment with the seriousness of his delivery, "what SUX^{2}BU actually *does*—and this will get me sued by a million lawyers and maybe assassinated, but it's a risk I have to take ..." He paused a moment.

"What it actually does ..."

He was too late. Sage was out the door with a quick step and an apologetic wave. *This is taking too long,* he thought. *I can find out about all this some other time.*

"... it collapses all the different selves back into the single being they came from," the scientist finished, eyes still closed and not noticing that he had lost his audience.

"I was working on a method of distribution, but for some reason it's spreading randomly, like a virus. I haven't worked that part out yet."

How embarrassing, thought Preisczech. He stopped. He had been too deliberate, too meticulous in trying to craft his words.

Sage was gone.

"Never mind," said Preisczech softly to himself.

It was okay. Look on the bright side. Nobody had understood him at *all* before he met Sage, and Sage at least partially understood.

CHAPTER THIRTY-FIVE

ROUNDING UP
THE CREW

The townspeople, townSquids, townbeasties, whoever, had grown used to seeing Edwin Puppy around the village, coming and going from the law office, tipping his hat to them on the street, picking up and returning things they had dropped, blessing them with his friendly greetings and the understated sunshine of his smile. They liked and trusted him. He was one of them now.

Thus it became the unenviable task of this same Lawyer Puppy—the increasingly real one living in Dry Creek Gulch, not the imaginary character in Gabriel Redborne's books—to contact all the prospective crew members and passengers and persuade them to go along on the Great Expedition. This might not be easy as they were scattered through time and space and some had actual jobs, while some were lazy and not easily talked into anything. He'd gotten stuck with this assignment because everyone else in town had been smart enough to avoid it.

Basel Vasselschnauzer could not go because his brilliant verbal abilities were purely negative. So the task fell to the most charming and persuasive individual any of them knew, an attorney to boot, and apparently with some free time on his hands.

His status was ambiguous enough to give some of the O.G. Dry Creek Gulchians pause.[35] It was not entirely clear whether he was a human or some sort of animal, though cases of such mixed status were not unheard of in the town—look at Jenny! And Squidress Four, for that matter. His status regarding the real vs. imaginary dichotomy was also in doubt. He had plenty of company in this as well, but there was nobody else who shared these *double* ambiguities. (It would make a lovely Venn diagram.)

Then there was the matter of defense attorney Edwin Puppy vs. county prosecutor Edward Youngdog. Was he one or the other? Or both? And if he was both, how in the world would he navigate the upcoming trial in which the two lawyers would act as opposing counsel?

So, Puppy possibly had some issues, but the group still considered him the best choice.

---

35 We're tempted to use the word paws, but the urgency of the task at hand precludes such silliness.

He decided to start with Jenny. She was kindly and welcoming, nurturing and sympathetic.[36]

PUPPY: Jenny, dear, would you like to come along on an exciting expedition to finally and decisively save the Multiverse?

JENNY: No thank you, I've seen all of the Multiverse I need to for the next few millennia. I'm happy right here. But thanks for thinking of me anyway.

She offered a conciliatory smile, a consolation prize. Next, he tried an inducement, something that might intrigue her and also appeal to her pride and her sporting instincts.

PUPPY: I understand your human one is not your only identity. Your extraordinary gifts and talents as an actual citizen of the wider Multiverse could be decisive in deciding the success or failure of this important mission!

While Jenny was kind and considerate, she was growing firmer as she got used to dealing with importunate Earthlings, who did not have the social niceties of the Squid. Not wanting to waste any more time on this nonsense, she assumed her Squid Empress

---

36 He thought she might be susceptible of his charm, whichever form he chose to assume. He arrived at the Dirty Dog Cafe at a strategic time between post-breakfast clean-up and pre-lunch prep.

form: eight feet tall, sparking blue, insanely beautiful and impressive even beyond the ordinary run of Squidren.

JENNY: NO!

Edwin Puppy exited the cafe hastily with his metaphorical tail between his metaphorical legs. Perhaps the firmness of a prosecutor might be preferable to the innocent charm of a defender for the next attempt. He had decided to try Deandra.

Edward Youngdog (*whose demeanor was distinctly more assertive than Puppy's, maybe even a little intimidating*) said, "Ms. Hollandaise, your presence is required on a mission of the utmost importance. The fate of the galaxy, nay that of the entire Multiverse—"

He got no further.

"Eff off, Puppy!" Deandra told the lawyer, easily seeing through his disguise. She had had a few run-ins with police, attorneys, and courtrooms in her time and was fond of none of them.

This was not going well. Puppy looked at the list that Vasselschnauzer had provided him. He needed to pick his next target carefully, because he knew himself well enough to realize that, without a success pretty soon to buoy his mood, he would deflate like a pricked balloon and his assignment would be dead in the water. He had cleaned up the list and excised the unnecessary 'ands'.[37] He thought he'd try the easiest one or two next to give himself confidence. Black checkmarks indicated leads he thought were worth pursuing.

His Reordered and Annotated Basel List

Cats & Squidresses from the House of Cats (incl. Jenny)	Head Squidress said no.
Deandra Hollendaise	A firm no!
Fifth Street Mofos and Dirty Dog Boys	Too many of them, start elsewhere.
Computer geeks	Ditto
Black Foam Ball of Ultimate Significance	Later. Who knows where it is, or even *what* it is?
Cuttlefish	Later. Same as above.
Leila Umm Nuri, Halycon Sage, and Ratbone (Black Thread Team)	√
No-Name Stupid.	√
Higher Authority & Non-Squid off-Earth aliens	Too far away and / or incomprehensible
Cat Fatty Lumpkin	
Nuri	
Squidren, Lol Bey & others	
TechieSquid	
Abdurraheem	
Sophie	
Preisczech	

---

37 "Good work!" says a passing Mad Grammarian.

He glanced over the un-annotated ones. The last of them were too intellectual, too complicated, or just too strange to be easily persuaded. He didn't really understand them.

That left Lol Bey and No-Name Stupid, originally grouped together, and one more. Squidren were a tough place to start, but he might have some luck with the horse. He liked horses and they generally liked him. And now it was down to the Black Thread Team, the metaphysical types who, for some reason, had survived his process of elimination thus far.

He suddenly noticed that Ruby wasn't on the list, and he thought this was strange considering her excellent coordination, quick intelligence, and utter unflappability. But nobody had seen her in a long time as far as he knew. Perhaps that was the reason.

To recap, the final possibilities were Stupid and the Black Thread Team: Leila Umm Nuri, Halycon Sage, and Ratbone. *Of course* Sage was going, no need to contact *him*.

Ratbone—another complicated, multi-layered intellectual. So, while he should be included, he was not the best choice for building Puppy's confidence as the next attempt.

Leila Umm Nuri though. The name meant "Mother of Nuri" and indeed, underlying her other capabilities, such as leading a truly kick-ass Sufi Ceremony of Divine Remembrance for a mix of humans and aliens, she was a welcoming, motherly soul. He would assume the modest, appealing character of Edwin Puppy, and it would be a lead pipe cinch.

⟞⟝

A while later …

EDWIN PUPPY: Greetings, horse, I come in peace.

What? thought No-Name Stupid. *What kind of weirdo is this? I heard he was a dog, but what dog in the world ever talks like that?* He paused a moment in thought. *Ah, got it!* thought Stupid. *It's because he thinks I'm an Indian pony. Because of Sage.*

All of Stupid's supercilious instincts were aroused. While he hadn't been aware of this until recently, a new understanding of his motel TV watching with Sage, as well as some recent conversations with Rap and Beaner, had alerted him to micro-aggressions.

Eff off, Puppy! said No-Name Stupid, not in words. It was perfectly understandable to Puppy, though. He got the absolute rejection of it, and with an embarrassed little bow, he took his leave.

Stupid felt a bit bad. Perhaps the clueless dog-man hadn't meant to be offensive.

Only one more chance: the kindly, empathetic Iraqi wife and mother, baker of cookies. Surely she would not refuse a poor, threadbare lawyer down on his luck. (Puppy adjusted his suit to look more rumpled, and ruffled his hair in a way that some ladies incomprehensibly found adorable.) But *Jenny* was a cookie maker too, and she'd turned him down flat. If he couldn't talk Leila into going along he was giving up. Enough was enough!

PUPPY: Mrs. Hussein?
LEILA (kindly): Just call me Umm Nuri. It means Nuri's Mom. We Muslimas don't take our husband's names.
PUPPY: Yes, ma'am. Well, I really need something, and at this point I think you're the only one who can help me.
LEILA: Yes?

Her encouraging tones made him feel hopeful. So did the fact that she gracefully gestured him into a kitchen chair, took off her floury apron, and sat down across from him.

PUPPY: I need people to go on an expedition of ultimate importance, a journey across the Multiverse to gather up all those who will come together *to save everything!*

He ended with a dramatic rise of his well-modulated voice.

"If just one far-seeing and influential person such as yourself says yes, I'm sure the rest will follow and we can save the Earth! And everything else," he added.

"Oh, dear," said Leila, "It's almost Nuri's birthday, and also I promised to bake for this big literary conference. And Abdurraheem needs a hand with his new invention, and if I leave, who will feed the poultry? I'm so sorry, Edwin, I just can't see my way clear to do this right now." "*Asif,*" she added again. "I'm sorry."

As he was walking out the door in defeat, Edwin Puppy realized that he had just received the courteous, foreign-lady equivalent of the same answer he'd gotten from Deandra Hollendaise and No-Name Stupid.

CHAPTER THIRTY-SIX

RUBY TAKES CHARGE

"You're kidding," said Ruby. "You mean they won't go? Nobody can get them to *go*?"

"Well, you know *I* can't do it," replied her old friend Basel Vasselschnauzer. (Might as well admit it, that was the relationship now.)

Really, his self-awareness was coming along beautifully. Except regarding literature, he used to have all the insight of a potted plant.

"Who did you send?" asked Ruby.

Vasselschnauzer felt a little guilty. If he had remained engaged with the project instead of washing his hands of it as soon as his list was done, he would have picked somebody more suited to the job than *Edwin Puppy*, for heaven's sake.

"This is stupid. I'll fix it," said Ruby. "*YO, SQUID!*" she shouted, both vocally and telepathically. There weren't necessarily any Squidren nearby, but that really didn't matter. One of them would pick this up.

TechieSquid blinked into existence a few feet away.

"Can you transmit a message for me, please?" asked Ruby. "We need to get this expedition organized so we can take off and get back before the literary conference."

TechieSquid was delighted. He was getting sick of hanging around the earthplane all the time and baby-sitting the SquidShip. *Woo hoo* and *yay*, it was time to be off!

"Listen up," called Ruby in her clear, commanding voice. Not a yell, but it certainly carried. "When you hear your name, go and pack anything you need for an extra-galactic journey. We'll be taking the SquidShip. You have 30 minutes."

Then she called the names of all the people, aliens, animals and groups on Basel's list and TechieSquid passed it on to them wherever they might be.

Two expressions that we've used before in The Sage Chronicles sum up the effect of this, so take your choice.

"Piece of cake!" or "Bob's your uncle!"[38]

---

38 "Lovely outdated slang. Speaking as a Mad Grammarian, I approve this message."

CHAPTER THIRTY-SEVEN

"GO GET THEM, TIGER[39]"

Dateline: We Really Don't Know.
Do We Have to Keep Doing This?

The idea of sending a magnificent expedition into the Greater Multiverse originated as a lazy attempt by K.V.B. to avoid work and bother. (We've told you she had many things in common with Halycon Sage and this tendency was one of them.)

There were characters in the first two books who had likely aroused interest; they had certainly aroused *hers*. To avoid dragging characters into the action who seemed to be saying, "No thanks, I'm done," and also to avoid questions starting with, "But what about," and "What happened to," and "I *really liked*," and "Why didn't you," she would merely gather up all the now superfluous

---

39 From one of Robert Monroe's out-of-body experience books, The Journeys Trilogy. This common phrase is usually rendered as, 'Go get 'em, Tiger," and for some reason we find the use of "them" here hilarious.

characters and send them off through hyperspace on some mission that she could doubtless make up later.

Problem solved!

But, not.

Because if you're a writer, or at least if you're a good one, you know that something you make up can sometimes lie there like a dead mackerel. K.V.B. had once offended a writer friend by sharing her comparison (which we read earlier) of an inspired versus an uninspired story to a living woman versus the same woman prepared professionally for burial, possibly equally beautiful, but still a corpse.

The friend thought this was a lurid exaggeration; we *don't*.

Karima's imam and spiritual adviser referred to the origin of endeavors like this as "The Bright Ideas Department." That is, the origin of things you think of by yourself without checking your inner guidance, resulting in enormous wasted time and energy as you go haring off after some idea that is basically crap. (Please pardon this mild swear.)

And just as some initially exciting ideas might turn out to be junk, the reverse can happen: Something thought up as a lazy work-around can unexpectedly turn *real*.

And the expedition, originally intended as work avoidance, had done just that! Had, in fact become the Last Desperate Attempt to Save Everything by Drawing Everybody In!

(You've never seen *that* before, haha.)

To quote Basel Vasselschnauzer quoting *The Wind in the Willows*, "A sword for the rat, a sword for the mole, a sword for the toad, a sword for the badger ..."

Everyone must be brought along and every resource made ready.

The great intergalactic, interdimensional journey to save the Multiverse is about to begin. *HERE WE GO!!!*

BUT FIRST ...

CHAPTER THIRTY-EIGHT

THE CONCLUDING ADVENTURES OF LAWYER PUPPY

**Puppy for the Defense!
Or, the Prosecution …**

Chapter Seven: Puppy Faces Himself

When we left Edwin Puppy, Esq., he had just stood up for the very first time as a practicing attorney in a real court of law to address the Bench. Of course, for the moment, he was appearing as his opponent and alter ego, representing the plaintiff.

"Who speaks for the County?" asked the judge.

"I do, Your Honor," said Edward Youngdog. (*Remember to call it the County, not the Plaintiff*, he reminded himself.)

"Assistant District Attorney Edward Youngdog for the County of Malagueña."

(Since this was Redborne's mini-novel and not real life, there was a bit of leeway in the matter of names. He though Malagueña sounded nice and the judge did not blink.)

"And who is representing the Defense?" asked His Honor calmly.

It was a question well worth asking. There was nobody at the defense table except the clients, who looked very prosperous but also exceedingly uncomfortable. Because their lawyer had not shown up.

"Will Mr. Puppy be joining us?" asked the judge sarcastically.

"Your Honor, may I approach the bench?" asked the young A.D.A.

"Help Yourself, Mr. Youngdog," said the judge with a sweeping, expansive gesture of his arm. Yes, he was one of those *sarcastic* judges.

Youngdog stepped up to the bench and spoke in a low voice, so low that we, who are transcribing these proceedings, could not hear what was said, which was probably just as well. However, a note came into our hands later which explains the situation.

TO WHOM IT MAY CONCERN: Judges presiding over courtrooms where Attys. Puppy and Youngdog are scheduled to appear have been made aware that both individuals have occasional bladder problems and have agreed to accommodate them in this matter.

Though this might seem embarrassing, it was actually a clever ploy devised by Puppy / Youngdog to let them dash out of the courtroom and change identities as needed.

"Very well. Mr. Youngdog, you may proceed with your opening statement," said the judge.

"Ladies and Gentlemen of the Jury," began Attorney Youngdog gesturing expansively toward the jury box. And then, just like magic, they were there, an intelligent, attentive-looking bunch representing a good variety of ages, ethnicities, and genders. It was so nice when things just worked themselves out without a lot of hassle. *There* are *some advantages to being a fictional character,* thought Youngdog to himself.

"The man you see before you, Mr. Elijah Davis, represents a group of 855 coal miners who have been stricken down by a devastating respiratory illness. None of them can breathe properly, most are unable to work regardless of their ages, and, sadly, a number have already died. Since Rattlesnake Mining, Inc. maintained unsafe conditions, avoided universally approved precautions, and is now attempting to evade its responsibility, we seek compensatory damages and extensive punitive damages for willful negligence. I rest my case.

One jury member turned to another. "Sounds reasonable to me," he said rather loudly. She nodded.

The judge banged his gavel half-heartedly, but didn't actually seem too interested.

"Excuse me a moment, Your Honor, Ladies and Gentlemen."

Youngdog raced out the door toward the red-carpeted and conveniently located restroom which he had cleverly scoped out a few days before.

But suddenly it was *gone!* He could not find it! (Probably because he was in the wrong courtroom.)

Puppy raced back and forth through the halls and corridors of the third floor of the courthouse, which was far larger than it had first appeared.

Beginning to panic, he dropped to the floor, suddenly manifesting a thick, shiny coat of curly black fur, four fine strong legs and a waving tail. He was quite a sight as he galloped up and down the hall. Ah, there it was at last!

Before a bank of shining mirrors, Youngdog stripped off his flamboyant red coat, outrageously large gold watch, horn-rimmed tortoise-shell glasses and the other accoutrements of his personality.

A few minutes later (because it took him a while to find it again), Edwin Puppy, Esq. returned to the courtroom.

"Puppy for the Defense, Your Honor," he exclaimed. (It was fun to say it out loud!)

"Please excuse the unavoidable delay. If it please the Court, I would like to combine my opening and closing statements and present them to the Jury."

"Aren't you going to call any witnesses, Lawyer Puppy?" inquired the judge, sounding slightly amused. "Opposing council did not seem to think it necessary."

"Witnesses! Yes, of course Your Honor. I call Mr. Forsyth Smythe-French to the stand."

"He's not going to go anywhere *else*, Mr. Puppy," remarked the judge. Oh, the pain that a sarcastic judge can inflict upon a sensitive young attorney! Puppy, now in fully human form, blushed a deep red.

The witness took the stand.[40] He was a middle-aged man and extremely well dressed.

"Do you see any reason why your company should not be fined and punished to the full extent of the law?" asked Edwin Puppy.

"Nope, sounds fair to me," replied the witness. "Hey, wait a minute, aren't you supposed to be defending us?"

This was a puzzler for Puppy, who had expended all his energy and ingenuity in developing his disguise and running up and down the hall looking for the bathroom.

"The Defense rests," he said, and added, being now quite rattled, "So does the Prosecution."

---

40 Where did he take it? I don't understand. Under-stand hahaha.

"The Plaintiff, Mr. Puppy," interpolated the sarcastic judge. "You mean the *Plaintiff*. Are you resting for *both* of you?"

Suddenly it was all too much.

"I can't do this, Your Honor, ladies and gentlemen of the jury. I've tried my best, but I'm trying to be two people at once, I slept through law school, and furthermore, *I'm fictional!* In fact, I'm *doubly fictional!* I am a character in a story within a story!" and finally his deepest, darkest secret burst passionately from his unwilling lips. "And I'm a *WEREPUPPY!!!*"

Gabriel Redborne smiled, wrote THE END, and put down his pen.

CHAPTER THIRTY-NINE

AN ABRUPT LEFT TURN

This wasn't really a left turn, you see, or only in a sort of metaphorical sense, but it was an unexpected lurch in an unexpected direction, so we'll leave this chapter title, which pleases us.

The order in which the writers would present themselves and read some of their work—in most cases, whole novels since the Post-Modernist Minimalist etc., etc., etc. novels were so *short*—had been carefully weighed and calibrated by the Select Committee, which consisted of Sophie McGregor, Basel Vasselschnauzer, and, to everybody's dismay, Niemand Kompt, who insisted on being part of this elite group and could not be kept away.

Halycon Sage should have been one of the decision makers, but he'd wanted nothing to do with it from the start, being temperamentally allergic to all forms of deliberate organization and management. Really, they were lucky he'd agreed to show up to the conference at all.

And while there had been no chance *ever* of his joining this committee, the presence of Kompt assured that he would be a thousand miles away, metaphorically if not physically. For the first time he felt the attractions of the ridiculously far future and the In-Between Space.

This being the case, Sophie and Basel were on their own, and they were stuck with Kompt, who sat there looking like a smug skeleton with his hollow cheeks and burning eyes. At last—at last!—he had succeeded in forcing Sage to notice him, even (during the projected conference program) to be in the same room with him for extended periods of time!

His triumph was absolute. He had wanted so badly to be a supervillain, to be Sage's nemesis and opposite number, and his failure had been spectacular.

But now, now, all the power in the world was in his hands. All the power in Dry Creek Gulch, which was apparently all that was *left* of the world. *All mine, mine, MINE,* he thought …

Woah. He stopped himself in mid-slide down into the dark pit of his former way of thinking. He could not fall into this trap again, for he really had learned something after the most recent End of the World, his total realization of his irredeemable evil, and his consummate failure.

At least he had *thought* they were irredeemable and consummate, and there in the timeless time between the detonation of atomic weapons and the miracle which allowed the Squidren and the Braided Thread Teams to walk the whole disaster back and save the world, he had sobbed and sobbed, cried his heart out, this man who had lived in the smug satisfaction of evil since early childhood, who had never doubted the rightness of his own toxic world view.

Seeing his futility, his apparently ultimate failure, he had asked one question of the Unnamable Force which had, from the heart of silence, solicited their questions. There seemed nothing to lose, though only a few had responded to this offer.

Out of his utter defeat came the question, "Does anybody love me?" and the answer had been a simple, "Yes." And after a brief, unmeasurable time, Halycon Sage had stepped over and given him a hug. This occurrence had surprised the presumed author Karima Vargas Bushnell and also the *other* presumed author, Halycon Sage. Only Karima's life partner of many decades had been unsurprised, saying he'd been expecting it.

So, now Kompt was a changed man, but not entirely redeemed, still having the habits of a lifetime to contend with. To Sage, and to those on the Literary Event Committee, he was still a consummate pain in the ass.

♾

Oh, dear, we notice that we never got to the point here, having been captured by the set-up. This change in the formerly evil and nihilist author, whose hideously depressing works went on for thousands and thousands of pages, hammering the reader in excruciating detail with the useless pointlessness of existence, was *not* the actual left turn.

The left turn had to do with the order in which the authors appeared and what happened at what should have been the climax of a successful conference, enabling everyone to grin and pat themselves on the back, add a line to their resumes, and go home conscious of a job well done.

The order of the speakers had been planned so carefully! First, Lydia Larchwood, young and innocent with her sweet stories of girlhood, adolescence and young womanhood, was bound to put the audience in a tolerant and sympathetic mood, relaxing and reassuring them and creating openness toward the more challenging and radical works to come. She was to read first *Pat the Cat*, then *The Girl with the Funny Name,* and then *Monday, Will You Marry Me?* She did, and made a nice job of it. So far everything was going as planned.

Next, to convince the audience that the conference would offer literary depth as well as soothing sweetness, Felicity Hagedorn assumed the stage, reading *The Snove* and the final two paragraphs of *What's in a Name?* Again, all went well. Those attending caught a glimpse of the challenging metaphysical depths to come, exploration of the very outer fringes of consciousness. Again, *check*. Mission accomplished.

There had been some disagreement between Sophie, Basel, and Kompt as to whether the speakers should be of alternating genders. Sophie, who was a post-post-feminist, and Basel who was apparently a bit gender fluid (though he still felt this was nobody's business), thought this didn't matter.

Perhaps unsurprisingly, the former aspiring supervillain was the one who thought there should be strict alternation—villains are sometimes very conservative—but he was voted down.

So, after Larchwood and Hagedorn—*what an excellent name for a law firm!* thought the passing Edwin Puppy, who had somehow picked up this thought.[41]

After Larchwood and Hagedorn, the next author was supposed to be Wade Garnette, Sensitive Macho Dude and author of westerns and other male-oriented, outdoor-inspired novels, reading *Baraboo Bartholomew, Fur Trapper with a Heart.*

Unfortunately Garnette, who as we have seen had an unexpected soft spot for animals and for pretty much everything and everybody else, had forgotten all about the conference and was a no-show.

As you may recall, he had begun to worry about whether his character Baraboo Bartholomew would lack

---

41 It was one of the strange and sometimes annoying features of Post-Event Dry Creek Gulch that almost everyone there, real, imaginary, or in between, had acquired some degree of psychic ability. You couldn't call your mind your own anymore.

for food. On one level, he knew the character was unreal, but these days imaginary characters in and around Dry Creek Gulch were stepping forward to claim personhood with alarming regularity. Why just look at Edwin Puppy, stepping off the page and opening an actual law office! Fatty Lumpkin was another example.

So, if these absurd characters could become real, why not Baraboo Bartholomew? The more Wade Garnette tried to put this thought out of his mind, the more it obsessed him, with the predictable result that, at the moment when he should have been assuming the stage and wowing the audience with the brevity and depth of his novel, he forgot the conference entirely and was at home with the random collection of rabbits, chickens, and other creatures he'd acquired since coming to town.

The Squidresses and others at The House of Cats where he was lodging tolerated his growing menagerie as long as he kept it to the large room he was renting, and the cats themselves had been unexpectedly benign and were sometimes allowed to come in and play.

Because Sage needed to be kept for last as the climax of the event, and because Kompt's works, *The Black Gray Dark*; *I'm Fabulous, You're a Necrotic Collection of Worm Food* and so on, were too long and depressing to come so early in the program, the next obvious speaker was Gabriel Redborne, who was sure to be a crowd pleaser with his scintillating Magical Realism Legal Thrillers.

Unfortunately, he was not there either. Nor was Halycon Sage.

They could not be found anywhere. (More about this later. Or before. You may have noticed that time has become quite fluid in the unfolding of this book.)

Sophie, wearing high heels for once and dressed to the nines, stepped onto the stage and calmly announced that there would be a fifteen-minute intermission and refreshments could be found in the lobby of the old hotel.

Sophie's composure vanished the moment she disappeared behind the red velvet curtain, where she signaled frantically to Emma, Leila, Preisczech, and Squidress Four.

While all of them were wonderful cooks, the original plan had been to send everyone to the Dirty Dog Cafe for lunch, but now Squidress Four stopped time for a couple of hours while they made assorted hors d'oeuvres, canapés, and little cakes and pies for the unexpected break.

Now the gender balance so dear to the heart of the surprisingly traditional supervillain was entirely eff'd. Because only one possible next speaker remained. A heated discussion was carried on in whispers in the green room under the stage.

SOPHIE: No! We can't. I won't *have* it!
KOMPT: We have no other choice. It will be alright. Surely
    we've faced trials more serious than this!
BASEL: It seems a bad idea. You know what she's like …
KOMPT: We have no other choice.

And for possibly the first time in his life, having spoken both briefly and reasonably, he had the satisfaction of feeling others bend to his will, not through threats and intimidation, but through sensible and even kindly persuasion.

A whole new world was opening up!

Sophie stepped back onto the stage and up to the (working) microphone.

"Our next author needs no introduction; we are proud to present Ms. Deandra Hollendaise."

Looking really quite beautiful, but still pretty much unbearable as a person, smirking, slinking, and almost slithering in her long, silky dress, the author of *The Pizza Pie's Wife* and *Claudia Fanghorn and the Alligator King* assumed the stage.

CHAPTER FORTY

THE PROGRAM

**Being the Exposition, Inquisition, Imposition,
and Supposition,
in short, an Intellectual Investigation
(and Feast for the Inquiring Mind)
into the Post-Modernist Minimalist
Neo-Symbolist Pseudo-Realist
School of Literature
with Founder Halycon Sage
And various Authors of Distinction within
the Various Branches of that School**

Convener and Chair: Sophie McGregor, Valedictorian
Dry Creek Gulch High School.

> <u>EDITORS' NOTE:</u> It was an Aggravation to Sophie that, there no longer being any Universities, she was not able to earn an MA or MS and ultimately a Ph.D. to list among her Credentials. (It is also to be noted that We, the Editorial Board of the Sage and Squid Publications Team, have Inadvertently Picked Up the Style and Unnecessary Capitalization that Characterizes Sophie Herself.)

Ahem. (No, that's not about sewing, it's a once common but now outmoded attempt to reproduce the sound of someone clearing their throat.)

A PASSING SQUID: I still don't get this. What is a 'throat', and how do you 'clear it'? Won't somebody please explain?

THE PROGRAM

The Officials

Convener and Conference Chair
Sophie McGregor, H.VA.

Founding Author and Keynote Speaker
Halycon Sage

Round Table Chair
Basel Vasselschnauzer, Ph.D.

Committee Member
Niemand Kompt

The Participating Authors

Deandra Hollendaise
Heaving Bodice Romance Division

Gabriel Redborne
Legal Eagle & Magical Realism Divisions

Lydia Larchwood
Young and Restless YA & Precocious Kids Divisions

Felicity Hagedorn
Literary Fiction Division

Wade Garnette
Sensitive Macho Dude Division (Western)

And Special Guests
Internationally Famous Authors
Halycon Sage ... ... and ... ... **Niemand Kompt**
Everybody who's anybody will be here!

WELCOME

As we've already seen, the phrasing of the final sentence was worrisome: to the townspeople, to visitors from outside the area, who were getting in more and more frequently, and to most of the attendant Squidren, especially TechieSquid, who could not leave it alone.

He kept worrying the idea like a human with a bit of gristle stuck in his/her/its/their teeth. Because *everybody* was *somebody!* And if you were somebody, surely you were also anybody, though of course you were not *everybody*. That went without saying. TechieSquid said it anyway, softly underneath his breath, or perhaps he just thought it loudly.

At any rate, Halycon Sage, who was seated a few chairs away in the front row, must have caught his soft mumble or loud thought, because he shot him a sympathetic glance and a quick telepathic flash. *I know, I had the same problem. Don't worry about it, it's just a lot of nonsense.*

But if somebody isn't anybody, persisted TechieSquid's monomaniacal mind, *who are they then? Aliens? But we're somebodies. Are they furniture? But even furniture has feelings.*

He could have gone on like this for hours, and sometimes had when he was alone on the SquidShip with no one for company but the sleeping tankful of Zi.

Fortunately, a new person entered the room, creating a diversion.

AND NOW ...

THE REAL ACTUAL LIVE AND IN PERSON
FIRST ANNUAL DRY CREEK GULCH LITERARY
CONFERENCE ON THE POST-MODERNIST
MINIMALIST NEO-SYMBOLIST PSEUDO-REALIST
SCHOOL OF LITERATURE
AND ITS EXCITING NEW AUTHORS

CHAPTER FORTY-ONE

THE READINGS BEGIN

The Authors

1. **Wade Garnette - *Baraboo Bartholomew, Fur Trapper with a Heart*** (WESTERN)

Wade Garnette, like Halycon Sage himself, roams the Southwest on an actual horse, lives close to the land, and does western-type stuff. But like most of us in these confusing, post-modern times, he is not entirely consistent, as his beautiful white stallion is named Aktolgali after the horse in the Turkish drama *Dirillis Ertugrul*, which he watched on Petflix. Mr. Garnette has a deep feeling for animals, as can been seen in this, his first novel. He may be one of the few vegetarians riding the rodeo circuit.

2. **Deandra Hollendaise - *Clawdia Fanghorn and the Alligator King, I, II & III*; *The Pizza Pie's Wife*; and *The Story of Gerund* (ROMANCE)**

We're certainly hearing *a lot* from Deandra Hollendaise lately! (Possibly too much.) Deandra is self-described in her novel *Clawdia Fanghorn Book I* as "beautiful Deandra Hollendaise tossing back her ~~red~~, ~~black~~, ~~ebony~~, crimson sea of long curling locks which curled like the sea." Her locks are also "silken." Her hand, her form, and everything else about her, are repeatedly described as "delicate." The grammatical joke at the heart of *The Story of Gerund* betrays more erudition than one would have suspected—perhaps she has hidden depths!

3. **Felicity Hagedorn - *The Snove* and *What's in a Name?* (LITERARY FICTION)**

Felicity Hagedorn is, by her own admission, supremely unnoticeable. Fiftyish, rather thin with fading brown-gray hair, there is nothing about her to draw your attention. All the better to observe and capture you (and everything else) with her insightful novels! Her inside knowledge would place her in Dry Creek Gulch, but none of our contacts there remember ever seeing her—unlike Ms. Hollendaise, who can be hard to avoid. Her powers of observation and psychological insight are something beyond the ordinary. We hope to hear more from Ms. Hagedorn!

4. Gabriel Redborne - Puppy for the Defense! Or the Prosecution ... (LEGAL THRILLER / MAGICAL REALISM)

From early childhood, Gabriel Redborne wanted to be a lawyer. Or a vet. Unfortunately, he couldn't decide which, and this problem persisted into adulthood. A passionate idealist, he flunked out of law school through his intense involvement with rescue animals. And while he loved caring for animals, he couldn't bear the thought of "putting them to sleep," or even giving them shots, so any career in the veterinary sciences was out. These agonizing dilemmas were captured in his longstanding diary, the basis for the character of Edwin Puppy.

5. Lydia Larchwood - *Pat the Cat* (KID'S LIT), *The Girl with the Funny Name* (YA), and *Monday, Will You Marry Me?* (ROMANCE)

We don't know much yet about Lydia Larchwood. She tells us her life has been relatively isolated and that her friends have been the thousands of books and two cats with which she shares a strange old house. She probably lives in Dry Creek Gulch—they all do, don't they?—but not even that is certain. The only thing we know for sure: Lydia Larchwood wrote her first novel, *Pat the Cat*, at a very early age.

First up was Lydia Larchwood, youngest of the new postmodernist authors at the age of 12. This was tossing her a softball so she could read her sweet little books and get off the stage to enjoy the rest of the day, including cotton candy and stuff.

The town's magnificent cooks—Leila, Emma, Jenny, and Preisczech—had figured out how to make cotton candy. Preisczech's scientific training had come in handy in devising work-arounds for many no-longer-existent technologies, like the cotton candy machine. And since the formerly Squid-induced barrier appeared to be increasingly breaking down, a lot more previously impossible stuff was getting in and becoming possible.

Lydia stood center stage behind the podium, wearing a purple 1950s-style kid dress and looking down modestly. But considering the size of the audience and how everyone else out-gunned her in both age and weight, she was remarkably calm. Because they did *not* out-gun her in intelligence!

She began to read:

Pat the Cat

Pat the Cat was the *name* of the cat, but it was also a direction, an order and a complete sentence, because her human found this funny. But her name was confusing for Pat the Cat because she herself could not *obey* the order very efficiently, so she supposed the direction was directed at whoever was *with* her.

The outcome of this was that Pat the Cat learned two skills. The first thing she learned was to pat herself on the shoulder or opposite arm or leg with her paw if no humans were around. (She could never teach the other animals to pat her, though some of them would nuzzle her in response to her repeated request—and this brings us to her second skill.)

Like quite a number of cats that can be seen in life and on YouTube, Pat the Cat could *talk*. (Fatty Lumpkin, an Orange Cat of whom you may have heard, had several times said, "Hello?" though he pronounced it "Hewwo?" not having the vocal equipment to make the 'L'.)

So Pat the Cat learned to speak one sentence, which obviously ended with a question mark. "Pat the Cat?" "Pat the Cat?" she would say. And people usually did. So that was alright.

The End

Her still-childish voice was low and sweet, but quite audible to the respectfully silent audience. (It was early in the day and they hadn't gotten into the home-brew yet.) The story was well received.

LYDIA: The mini-novel you've just heard comes from the Precocious Kids' Division of the Post-Modernist Minimalist Neo-Symbolist Pseudo-Realist School of Literature, and actually I wrote it when I was *nine*. As I'm twelve now, I want to offer an example of slightly more mature writing, this one belonging to the Young & Restless YA Division.

She cleared her throat and read.

CHAPTER FORTY-TWO

THE READINGS CONTINUE

The Girl With The Funny Name

by Lydia Larchwood

Raised by a third-generation hippie mother on an isolated rural commune, she had no idea what she would face when she joined the real world.

The odd looks and double takes.

Sitting alone in the high school cafeteria.

The sneers, the snide remarks, and the outright laughter.

It wasn't her long, straight hair parted in the middle, or her oddly long skirts and 100% cotton clothing—all made at home, of course. It wasn't even her old-fashioned way of talking, like "far out," and "bummer."

She could not really blame her traditionally minded mother for naming her after two great-grandmothers who had kept bees and worked the land. They were admirable women.

But still …

Could a girl called Polly Esther ever find happiness?

The End

LYDIA: I wrote that one when I was eleven. But this last selection was written this year, and at the age of 12, I would be accepted into society as an adult in a number of cultures. So right now here in front of you, I am making so bold as to suggest its inclusion in the Heaving Bodice Romance Division. Though I personally don't see how a bodice can throw up.

(She reads.)

Monday, Will You Marry Me?

by Lydia Larchwood

It was very confusing, you see. Because her *name* was Monday. She was a pretty girl with a long brown ponytail and sparkling brown eyes, but not so pretty that total strangers would normally propose to her on the bus.

So when she heard the words, "Monday, will you marry me?" she knew that this was true love at last! Turning with a saucy toss of her head, she faced the handsome young man seated behind her, threw caution to the winds, said, "Yes, I will!"

The man seemed taken aback. He looked at her with embarrassment.

"Er," he said, "I wasn't talking to *you*."

Were five more shocking words ever spoken? No, they were not.

But Monday, with great presence of mind, tossed her ponytail again and said, "Well, I wasn't talking to you either!"

"I was talking to my girlfriend," he went on, indicating the blonde beside him. A blonde, what a surprise. "We've been trying to decide what day to get married."

"I'm sure it's of no concern to me," said Monday coldly, turning away.

At which point her eyes met the eyes of the tall young man seated across the aisle, his own black eyes glittering with amusement. He had overheard the whole thing.

How embarrassing.

Yet somehow, how delightful. His glittering black eyes and her sparkling brown ones met in a mutual glimmer of understanding.

Perhaps this day would not turn out so bad after all.

The End

This time the applause was enthusiastic, not to say uproarious! (Somebody had found and tapped the keg, and mugs and canteens of the stuff were going around. That might have been a contributing factor, though the Dry Creek Gulchians' appreciation was genuine.) And her romance novel, unbeknownst to her, actually *had* been included in the program.

Now there stepped onto the stage a nondescript 50-ish woman who seemed not to have bothered at all with her appearance for this important event.

She's not wearing any make-up—did she even comb her hair? thought the exasperated Deandra Hollendaise, who herself had spent many hours getting ready.

But nobody else seemed to mind.

Felicity Hagedorn cleared her throat and began to read:

THE SNOVE

by Felicity Hagedorn

The Snove was not happy. Originally generated from undifferentiated reality by a quaint and momentary mispronunciation on the part of a householder, the Snove had somehow attained self-awareness, and a small degree of agency. But not enough—hence, the Snove was Grumpy. Not just as a temporary state; at least at its inception, Grumpiness was the defining characteristic of the Snove, the nexus of its personality.

Perhaps it had taken a leaf from the Nanobots' book,[42] beginning as an invented object for the utility of Man (or in this case, possibly of Woman), then unexpectedly acquiring sentience. So, yes, it started out as a stove. An old, rather battered, very greasy, and extremely ordinary electric stove.

But the Snove, newly born, had *thoughts* and *feelings* and wanted to be recognized as an independent entity. It wanted to express itself, to be acknowledged, and most of all, *it wanted to walk around.*

---

42 This is an expression. As far as we know, the Nanobots have never written an actual book, and a good thing, too! If they did, it would be monumentally long and boring, with them being obsessive machines and not all that smart if you want the truth. And besides, how would all the authors come to agreement on anything? There are billions of them!

It had become obsessed with The Living Room, which it heard about daily, but had never seen. *What's going on out there?* it wondered. *What is a Living Room, and who or what lives there? What do they do in it? What are they saying? Do they ever talk about* Me?

Someday, somehow, it was determined to go there.

The End

Felicity Hagedorn had also been invited to read the very end of her other novel, *What's in a Name?* It follows the struggles and eventual success of two teenaged musicians named, respectively, Ollie and Ali, which commonality leads to predictable and formulaic confusion. Aside from the setup and the ending, the book focuses almost exclusively on their discussions of the remarkable similarities between their quirky personalities.

("Yawn," was the terse comment offered by Niemand Kompt, and the other two could not but agree.)

The young musicians, floundering around trying to decide on a band name, at last came up with the following scenario, which even the bored and exacting Committee members had to agree was pretty good, or at least worth reading.

Felicity cleared her throat and offered a brief synopsis of the plot summing up everything the audience would be missing by not hearing the whole book. (Truth to tell, reading them the entire book would probably have taken less time than the brief synopsis.)

Ms. Hagedorn looked around at the waiting crowd, cleared her throat, and began.

A Reading from the Final Sequence of *What's in a Name?*

Then genius struck: They decided to call their band after the *third* thing they had in common: an undiagnosed but marked tendency to OCD. Their oddities included eating food in alphabetical order, straightening carpet fringe multiple times a day, and being unable to practice with the closet door open, even a crack. They also worried pretty much all the time, about pretty much everything. Each thought gave birth to ten more thoughts and each of those to a hundred. So they found at last the perfect name, a name with a nice post-punk, heavy metal sound, just a bit dark and intellectual.

They were **CHAINS OF RUMINATION.**

Only one band in Dry Creek Gulch posed any challenge to them at all, but this band was dynamite. From its name you'd have thought the members were a bunch of idiots, but actually these young ladies were brilliant and daring, both musically and intellectually. Only the most self-confident of teenagers would have dared to call themselves

THE SIMPERING NINNIES.

The End

CHAPTER FORTY-THREE

A MINOR PANIC

It was at this moment that the Left Turn was discovered, the situation you may recall from earlier in this saga in which several critical authors failed to appear as scheduled.

SOPHIE: Where's Wade Garnette? He's supposed to be next.
BASEL: No idea. I haven't seen him this morning.
KOMPT: I don't see Sage around either. Maybe I'd better go next. *The Black Gray Dark* will lend a hitherto-missing seriousness, even gravitas to this event, and—
SOPHIE AND BASEL: *NO!*

EDITORS' NOTE: Fearing panic and rebellion within the small committee, Sophie took charge. Her practical intelligence and decisive personality made her the natural leader of almost any group.

SOPHIE: Let's get Gabriel Redborne up there. His stuff is good, and Niemand, he'll fulfill the gender balance thing you were so concerned about.

They looked around the packed auditorium.

EDITORS' NOTE: *Auditorium now?* Sure, why not. Everything in Dry Creek Gulch is becoming fluid, adapting itself to meet the needs of the moment.

But Gabriel Redborne was *also* nowhere to be seen, and the audience, though fueled with beer and the success of the program so far, was becoming restive.

BASEL (Trying not to panic): What do we *do?*

KOMPT: In this emergency, I'd be glad to—

SOPHIE AND BASEL: *NO!*

SOPHIE: Let's get Deandra up there. She's really the only choice we have. Unless you'd like me to read one of my research papers on the Squidren—

At this point, her two colleagues reluctantly acquiesced, and Deandra was called to the stage.

CHAPTER FORTY-FOUR

DEANDRA READS

Diandra Hollendaise stepped onto the stage and up to the podium. As usual, her beauty and fashion sense were beyond dispute. Her long dress, both flowing and clinging, featured exquisite colors, in fact the very dark blue and turquoise combination so loved by the Squidren, along with the daring addition of some magenta.[43]

Also, as usual, the effect was mostly spoiled by her obvious conceit and condescending attitude, the product of her cluelessness that there was any system of values other than her own.

However reluctantly though, we must acknowledge her undoubted creativity. Quite a number of beings, on

---

43 We make a quick and unobtrusive SquidSign here, in case anyone should be offended; we all know how the Squidren feel about magenta! (Except the Zi of course, but that's a whole different bag of cats, and we're not getting into it right now.)

Earth and off, are enjoying The Heaving Bodice Romance Division of the Post-Modernist Minimalist Neo-Symbolist Pseudo-Realist School of Literature, of which she is the undoubted founder and pioneer.

> EDITORS' NOTE: Warning: This will be rather long (but *good!*). Those of you with short attention spans, please do not disrupt the flow of the reading. You can go out to the lobby and get another beer if necessary.

DEANDRA READS:

Clawdia Fanghorn and the Alligator King

Book I

By Deandra Hollendaise

"**N**o, *no*, Clawdia Fanghorn, stop *biting* me!" said the beautiful Deandra Hollendaise tossing back her ~~red black ebony~~ crimson sea of long curling locks which curled like the sea.

The great, silken Redcat paid no attention, continuing to take tiny, delicate bites at the delicate hand which held the pen which was trying to write a new novel.*

"*Stop it!*" reiterated Deandra, sweeping back her silken locks with her other delicate hand in annoyance.

Clawdia Fanghorn responded by using her long, sharp claws like a pair of tong-shaped salad servers to capture the delicate hand that tried to unsuccessfully shy away from her thorny grasp.**

"That's *it!*" fumed the beautiful Deandra. "I'm going to take you for a *walk*. To the *bottom* of the *garden*."

They lived in Louisiana, and along the bottom of the public garden at the end of the street, there flowed a deep creek. Who knew what lurked within those darkling depths? No one. But there had been rumors.

"Yes, *the bottom of the garden*," she repeated firmly, hoisting the great, furry, rug-like Redcat whose sweet, pale pink nose and pretty pale pink paw pads were so terribly deceptive, and whose pale green feline green eyes watched her ~~like a cat watching a mouse.~~ warily.

The tone of her delicate voice was *onimous*.

The End

---

* This was the first time she had ever put herself into one of her own books, but since Halycon Sage and Karima what's-her-name were doing it, it looked like it might be a *thing*.

** Editor's Note: Ms. Hollendaise would have used "pincer move" instead of "salad servers," but she is unfamiliar with the concept, not having read any war books. (How did this get in here? Never mind. Time & Space. Deandra can't see it, though, which is good.)

*** ~~If that stuck-up Ruby who thinks she's so fantastic can be called "the beautiful," then *so can I!* Note to self: Delete this.~~

Book II

In his secret darkling lair at the bottom of the deep, dark, stagnant, swiftly-flowing creek, the Alligator King waited. His reptilian eye was open [Wait, are their eyes open or closed under water? If they're open, how do they *see?* If they're closed, how do they catch any fish or turtles or anything? Note to self: Check library. Wish the stupid internet wasn't fried.]

His reptilian eye was open as he watched with his ancient crocodile smile, smiling at the thought of the innocent creatures awaiting the onslaught of his evil teeth.

He was the biggest alligator ever seen—or *not* seen. In truth, he was a throwback to the dinosaurs, a true dinosaur. He was a *dinosaur*.

But nobody had ever gotten the best of Clawdia Fanghorn.

The End

Book III

i

The lovely and delicate Deandra Hollendaise had well and truly had it with Clawdia Fanghorn. Sure, she loved the troublesome feline, but she was tired of being bitten and scratched and lobstered, with scratches covering her delicate arms. Okay, so the bites were tiny and didn't really hurt, but it just wasn't *right!*

So a week after she made her threat, she actually grabbed the great ruggy Redcat firmly in her delicate arms and carried her all the way to that onimous place, the dark, deep, stagnant, and swiftly flowing creek at the bottom of the public garden!

She probably would not have actually thrown her *in*, but at the perfect psychological moment—well, not psychological, *physical* moment—Clawdia made a break for freedom and hurled herself into the deepest pool of that forbidding creek.

"Oh, *no*, Clawdia, I didn't really *mean* it," cried Deandra in deep distress! "I just wanted to scare you into being a better *cat!*"

But it was too late.

ii

There was a sudden ~~roiling~~ in the water, ~~boiling~~ in the water, ~~roiling in the boiling water~~ disturbance to the smoothly-flowing waters of Alligator Creek. And the huge dinosaur-like beast came thrashing to the surface, thrashing his tail like a maddened dinosaur.

The great jaws opened and snapped, but Clawdia was too quick! Seeming to leap above the surface of the water, she twisted nimbly in the air and landed on the Alligator King's back! Maddened with rage, he thrashed and twisted *himself*, attempting to dislodge this maddening creature who clung so firmly to his back, digging her sharp claws into his antediluvian scales! The water roiled with the boiling rage of their titanic battle! Never before had anyone defied the Alligator King, master of all he surveyed.

"Yowl mert *pert!*" said Clawdia. (Clawdia was a talker. She had an enormous vocabulary of interesting and funny sounds and could always be counted on to greet and take her leave politely upon entering or leaving a room. Plus, when she jumped down from anywhere, she always made a loud sound like a squeaky toy being thrown to the ground by a petulant child.)

These sounds were, Deandra realized belatedly too late, one of the reasons why she loved Clawdia Fanghorn. And yes, now that it was *too late*, she realized that she *loved* Clawdia Fanghorn! She loved her, but now it was too late!

"Oh woe is me!" cried Deandra, casting her lovely, delicate form disconsolately onto the grassy bank beside the creek in a paroxysm of sorrow and regret. "If only I had never come here! *If only!*" But the surface of the creek was suddenly, onimously silent.

iii

The Alligator King was tired. He had been trying for many minutes to dislodge the maddening, beautiful creature on his back, but he had no luck. He tried to snap her in half, but his fangy jaws could not reach and he merely gave himself a back spasm. He rolled over and over trying to drown her, but she just ~~leaped lept~~ leapt nimbly to his back again, like one of those log-rolling demonstrations.

The Alligator King paused in his machinations. Though he would have been panting if alligators could pant, still he was certain he could catch her in the end.

But it seems rather a pity, thought the winded Alligator.

"Pert?" asked Clawdia Fanghorn inquiringly. Could she read his *mind?*

She's just the right size for an appetizer, and would make a delightful mouthful indeed, he reflected. It almost seemed a pity, though. Her golden orange fur sparkled in the reflected sunlight off the water. She was a pretty creature, and spirited.

"Your fangs are very fine, my dear," said the Alligator King.

"I believe they have been admired, sir," she responded, modestly dipping her head. This behavior would have astounded those who knew her. It was out of character for Clawdia Fanghorn to defer to anybody.

"And your claws are sharp indeed," continued the monarch. "You use them in a peculiarly skillful way. It reminds me of something I have seen in the water, though exactly *what* escapes me ..."

"My mistress calls it 'lobstering'," replied Ms. Fanghorn modestly, flexing her long sharp claws.

"Perhaps I will not eat you today," responded the Alligator King. "You amuse me, and amusement is rare here in this swamp. Well, all my food is *rare*," he added with a dry little chuckle. "Excuse me," he added hastily, "What I meant to say is that we must talk again."

"Very well, Your Majesty," said Clawdia with a deep, feline bow of remarkable grace, and she made her exit.

Perhaps I will eat him first, she thought to herself with satisfaction as she made her way homeward. *The reptile may not be as smart as he thinks he is.*

Yet there was something about him. She had not before met a character so strong, so determined. And the somewhat elevated rhythm of the beating of her little catheart indicated that perhaps there was more than one emotion stirring within her feline breast.

To be continued ...

NOTE: The following was not supposed to be included in the reading, but apparently despite her appearance of calm, Deandra was a little nervous. At any rate, she read it, not knowing how to stop once she had begun. This unintended coda to her novel caused hilarity and raucous cheering from the audience, not only from the beer drinkers, but from everybody.

FROM: The Editors
TO: Ms. Deandra Hollendaise
Madam:
We regret to inform you that the length of this effort precludes its publication by our offices. It is simply too long, and no longer qualifies as a mini-novel. We wish you luck in your next endeavor.

Cordially,
The Editors

The End

Stupid Squid! thought Deandra, though in fact the Editorial Board was made up of many types of beings. But like Clawdia Fanghorn, Deandra was not to be beaten. She would never give up.

CHAPTER FORTY-FIVE

IN THE COURT OF THE MULTIVERSE, PART TWO

For those of you who've developed an affection for Lawyer Puppy and were sorry to see his story end, we have some good news.

While Gabriel Redborne's book and streaming series *Puppy for the Defense! Or the Prosecution …* is ended and with it, its doubly imaginary protagonist, the existence and even the legal career of the one-level-less-imaginary Edwin Puppy, Esq. now living in Dry Creek Gulch is far from over.

Since the third floor of the imaginary Malagueña County Courthouse is no longer available to him, Lawyer Puppy has transcended into far wider spheres and is, in fact, appearing before Judge Rumblethunder in the Intergalactic Time-Loose Actual Justice for All Beings

Court House even as we speak. We join the docket in progress.

CLERK: Call the case of Multiverse vs. Jane Deere.
EDWIN PUPPY (forgetting himself): What in the Name of Pants is that?
JUDGE RUMBLETHUNDER: Mr. Puppy, you forget yourself!

[Mr. Puppy did occasionally forget himself, being at least partially an actual puppy, but he had not forgotten himself on the carpet and faced the newspaper to the nose in weeks!

He found the accusation hurtful, in poor taste, and manifestly unfair and wondered silently if this were grounds for overturning the case on appeal. He had once overturned a case of oranges on a banana peel and suffered the paper to the nose combination, but that was neither here nor there.]

FATTY LUMPKIN (stepping in quickly to save his Learned Friend embarrassment): F. Atty. Lumpkin for the prosecution Your Honor, requesting a sidebar. Besides some confusion surrounding the proper designation of Defendant, a jurisdictional issue has arisen. There is some doubt as to whether Defendant can, in fact, be tried in this Court.

(Edwin Puppy digs through his briefcase, apparently looking for a particular set of papers. There is a prolonged

and disruptive rustling, scrabbling noise. Now Puppy appears to be trying to bury something under the papers.)[44]

JUDGE: You may approach the bench.

The bench was newly painted a lovely dark green and would have graced any park or outdoor space. Knowledge within the wider Multiverse of Planet Earth's legal protocols, which were being followed in this case since both attorneys and several parties were *from* that planet, is incomplete: extensive, but containing odd gaps.

Though the judge had been intending a sidebar, a quiet conference at the bench between himself and the attorneys, it quickly became apparent that everyone could hear everything anyway.

JUDGE: Counselors, I've changed my mind. Please be seated. Let us first deal with the matter of Defendant's identity and official designation within these proceedings. Madame Clerk, you say she is to be identified as Jane Deere, is that correct?

COURT CLERK: It is, Your Honor.

JUDGE: Are you sure you don't mean Jane Dear, that is, someone named Jane who is precious to and cherished by someone of importance to this case? Shall the clerk amend the name of the Defendant to Jane Dear?

PUPPY: No, Your Honor. Respectfully.

---

44 We have no clue as to what Puppy thinks he is doing at this moment. And the chances are that no one here will ever find out.

COURT REPORTER (In an undertone to the Judge): Your Honor, I believe the correct term is *Jane Eyre*, based on three pieces of information: First, Defendant has spent time on Planet Earth and is currently domiciled there. She is also close to a number of literary figures, and Jane Eyre is well known in Earthean literature. Although Defendant is very dear to one A. P., an Earthling who has been influential in affecting the wider Multiverse. So perhaps there is a case for …

INTERRUPTION: I believe *Jane Deere* is in fact the correct spelling, Your Honor, on the basis that Jane is a female form of the name John and John Deere is a well-known brand of tractor ubiquitous on Planet Earth.

ANOTHER INTERRUPTION: Except that this vehicle is used in farming country, such as the Midwest, while the locus of action regarding this case is *ranch* country, an entirely different place and located for our purposes in the *Far* West.

YET ANOTHER INTERRUPTION: Since the name Jane is indeed the female equivalent of the common name John, and there is a type of rejection letter known as a Dear John Letter—

SOMEBODY: That's called ghosting these days.

SOMEBODY ELSE: What days? Are we not outside the time space continuum? And what's a day, anyway?

SOMEBODY: Merely a figure of speech, my dear fellow.

INTERRUPTER: Your Honor, I believe every one of you has this all wrong.

JUDGE: And who exactly are you?

INTERRUPTER: I'm not exactly anybody, but I have special knowledge of Planet Earth and also pertinent information regarding the Defendant. She is a cook and—mark *this*—*a baker!* Therefore, since anonymous defendants are commonly called Jane or John Doe, this defendant, not being a deer, which is a delicate woodland animal, ought to be called *Jane Dough!*

The courtroom explodes in laughter and shouts of outraged decorum.

JUDGE (Pounding his gavel): Order in the court! Order in the court!

SOME SMARTASS: I'll have the ham and cheese.

THREE OR FOUR PEOPLE: I object!

JUDGE: *I* object! We're supposed to be starting a trial here, and there is no place for irrelevant interpolations from stupid and pun-making busybodies. The next person who interrupts these proceedings will be held in contempt!

All fall silent.

JUDGE: We order that, until such time as this matter is cleared up, the anonymous defendant shall be known simply as Jane.

Take half a parsec[45], and please return promptly.

---

45 Obviously a parsec is a unit of distance, not of time, and Judge Rumblethunder would surely have known this. Thus we can only assume a transcription error or perhaps malicious interference by the Snrrr.

CLERK: All rise.

The Adequately Magnificent Presence, a.k.a. Judge Rumblethunder, flowed majestically out of the courtroom taking his tank with him. It was certainly some sort of telekinesis, but not even those closest to him could ever figure out how he did it.

CHAPTER FORTY-SIX

SOME SPECIAL INFORMATION

efore we entirely adjourn and take a nice break, including for you, the reader, we must draw your attention to what may be the crux of this whole situation.

You may not have noticed, amid the recent downpour of objections and profuse detail, that some new facts were revealed about the Defendant. To wit: She is a baker, she is at present domiciled in the western part of a continent on Planet Earth, and she is dear to one referred to discretely by the Court Reporter as A.P.

All this leads us to conclude that the spelling of Defendant's *last* name is irrelevant and immaterial, while the real issue is the spelling of her *first* name. It is not unreasonable to suppose that aliens from a galaxy and dimensional level far distant from 2020s Planet Earth would not see a great difference between the name *Jane* and the name *Jenny*.

The court stood in recess for a brief time while the parties, attorneys, witnesses, and other attendees gathered in a nearby room for hot coffee or tea, little bowls of light, delicate bugs in seaweed, home-made chocolate chip cookies, and whatever else would add to their comfort and self-confidence in this rather stressful situation, appearing before the highest court in anywhere at all.

One would almost have sensed the guiding hand (tentacle) of Squidress Four (a.k.a. Miss O'Connell), that ubiquitous smoother of diplomatic waters, lately both a spy for the Squidren and second in command to author Rupert Griffin, founder of UnVirtual Time Travel, Inc.

One might *also* have thought that Leila, Emma, Squid Empress Jenny, and even Preisczech were assisting her. The food and the welcoming comfort were *that good*. This was important in a situation where worlds and universes hung in the balance and a moment of nervousness on the part of an attorney or an expert witness could make or break a case.

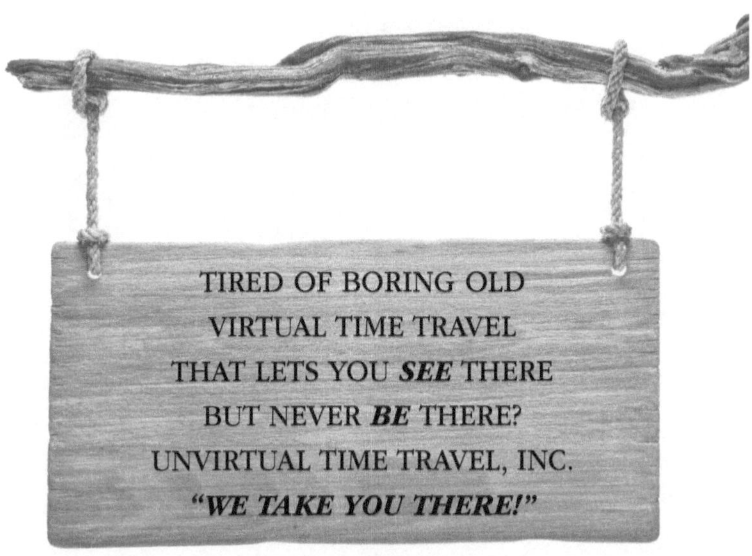
TIRED OF BORING OLD
VIRTUAL TIME TRAVEL
THAT LETS YOU *SEE* THERE
BUT NEVER *BE* THERE?
UNVIRTUAL TIME TRAVEL, INC.
"WE TAKE YOU THERE!"

CHAPTER FORTY-SEVEN

WHAT HAPPENED ON THE SQUIDSHIP

"'m starting to think there's a stowaway on this ship," said SquidSquad Commander Kennedy to himself in an undertone. "Maybe two."

"Oh, at *least* two!" responded Rupert Griffin, laughing a little because he himself was one of the stowaways, now stepping out of hiding for the first time. Griffin, celebrated author, academic, and founder of UnVirtual Time Travel, Inc., was an old friend of Commander Kennedy from the *last* time they'd had to save the Multiverse.

"So, who *are* these stowaways?" asked Kennedy automatically. "Great to see you!" he added as he realized who had just appeared.

While it was the Commander's job to keep order and discipline, he was so pleased to see his friend again that this no longer mattered, at least for the moment. Without Griffin, the Squids and fellow travelers could have been facing an exceedingly long and boring trip!

While the Squidren could get to most places instantaneously, not everyone on the ship had that ability, and this destination was farther than any of them had ever been. But now it would be *fun!* And not only would the Commander be diverted with interesting discussions, but the Squids could take a quicker-than-usual shortcut through time, should that be necessary.

"So, how are you? And how's UnVirtual Time Travel?" asked Kennedy conversationally.

Griffin attempted a Squidlike shrug, hard to do with only two pathetic arms. His friend felt sorry for him and looked away.

"Oh, not bad, everything's chugging along. But I was getting a little bored with time travel. I've been almost every*when*, but hardly any*where*."

"Well, I'm glad to have you on board," said the Commander. "Miss O'Connell?" he added in a louder voice. "Can you 'rustle up some grub' as they so quaintly say in western North America?"

"I don't think anyone says that anymore," replied Squidress Four. "And please remember that I was only Miss O'Connell and your assistant as part of my undercover spying activities.

"But I still have an interest in diplomatic catering and I *do* know the layout of the SquidShip," she added, relenting a bit. "So, if you'd like I'll see what I can do."

"That would be greatly appreciated, Squidress," replied the Commander humbly.

"So, who are the *other* stowaways on the ship? Do you know?" he asked again, turning back to his friend.

"Well, I saw a guy with two heads walking around. I don't know if *he's* supposed to be here."

Kennedy was about to explain about the part-Chillidian Squid, but Griffin was going on.

"Is Sage onboard?"

"Who knows?" responded Kennedy with a sigh. "I think he's popping in and out. You know how *Sage* is."

The two exchanged understanding looks.

"And the author Gabriel Redborne is here. He was supposed to speak at some conference in Dry Creek Gulch, but he said he was exhausted after finishing *Puppy for the Defense* and needed a rest."

"Well, based on his streaming show I'd say he's a probably good guy," responded Griffin, who was a fan. "But there's another stowaway you might want to be a bit concerned about, or at least be aware of. I saw him hiding in a dark corner listening, which seems to be kind of his *thing* if I remember correctly."

And suddenly right there before them stood former supervillain and nihilist author Niemand Kompt. He looked slightly less horrendous than formerly, though. There was something different about him.

"Hi," said Neimand Kompt.

Suddenly there was shouting in one of the hallways.

While the SquidShip was still on the Open Plan, it had been slightly redesigned and now contained more corridors as well as a greatly expanded Squidpool. There were more Zi onboard than formerly, necessitating a larger pool; this was their hangout and party room, though others were sometimes allowed in.

Since their enthusiastic reception by the Earthlings of Dry Creek Gulch, the Zi were being treated better by their fellow Squidren. Finding out that the Earthlings thought the Squids' problem with the Zi was about *gender* rather than *color*—the shocking and heretical acceptance of the higher-spectrum colors magenta, purple, and violet—had rocked the other Squids and perhaps opened some minds. It was strange to see that something which aroused fear and deep dislike in one place could seem positive or meaningless somewhere else.

A NOTE FROM THE SQUIDREN: Some of you reading this might be surprised that alien races like the Squidren, the Chillidians, the Snrrrr, and whatever grouping Judge Rumblethunder belongs to could be so naive and clueless about things any adult Earther would know.

But what you haven't taken into account is the many *other* spectra on their radar screens and the grades of differentiation within them which are wholly unknown to you.

EDITORS' NOTE: They may be paying close attention, and may even have constructed exact and sophisticated sciences, based on things you have never dreamed of. How many of you, for instance, could detect the subtle differences in vibrations between and within the *qigot*, *qibighot, shgwaqat,* and *hiermaghat* and a thousand other variations? Yet every Squid past babyhood knows this and could probably write and present a paper on it if called upon to do so.

[Our little disquisition on extra-galactic cultural differences is suddenly interrupted by even louder and nearer shouting.]

"What on *Earth?*" exclaimed Commander Kennedy, using an idiom for expressing surprise that he'd picked up in his most recent posting. It was, of course, entirely inappropriate to their current location halfway into the middle of hyperspace.

"It's *unnatural! Lavender, magenta, violet,* and all such colors from the supposedly 'higher spectrum' are against nature, against what is right and proper, against the way things ought to be. And throughout history, the vast majority of Squidren have agreed!"

Oh, ten heads in the water, thought Kennedy. *Is this anti-Zi garbage breaking out again?*

The Zi were too smart, that was the problem, and some of the more traditional Squidren couldn't handle it.

"Why else did we conceal the Zi when we first came to Earth?" continued the shouter.

"Why did we reveal them only in the most desperate moment when there was no alternative?"

This is not the Squidish way! thought Kennedy. Even when exhibiting ignorant attitudes, the Squidren were usually understated and polite. He was grateful that Obiwan Muhammad had not come along on the trip because she would have been deeply shocked and her new novel might have been affected.

Having passed the inflection point where, in about half of all possible realities, she had fallen victim to the Great Barbecue Conspiracy and died a hideous death, Obiwan was considered just about the most brilliant Squidish writer in the Multiverse.

"I further ask you, why did we only let them out of the Squidpool to be seen by the HooMans when there was literally no alternative?" went on the loud and bullying voice.

"Just in time to save your stupid butts," murmured Ratbone *sotto vocce*.

"What a pompous windbag," replied Halycon Sage with equal softness. "I'm not sure he's using 'literally' right either. It could be okay I guess ..."

Sage and Ratbone had taken refuge in a dark corner when the ranting started. The Squidren rarely got angry, but when they did, you did not want to be around. The two men's attention to the high decibel craziness was slightly distracted by the discovery that Niemand Kompt was in the corner with them.

"Hi," said Niemand Kompt again.

As an aspiring and at times highly successful supervillain and also as an even bigger literary snob than Basel Vasselschnauzer, he had never had occasion to *use* this word before; in his new life, he had grown fond of it.

Sage groaned and buried his face in his hands. He realized it was quite possible that Kompt had backslid and had come to kill him, but in fact Kompt only wanted to talk about the different types of participles and their use in literary fiction and to possibly share a boring explanation of the *tah marbuta* in Arabic. (Sage knew all about the *tah marbuta*, thank you very much. Probably more about it than the bragging pseudointellectual Kompt.)

He sat back and resigned himself to a couple of hours in the other author's company. He'd dealt with worse people, he supposed, and they *did* have some stuff in common. Who knew, perhaps they could even be friends.

Augustus T. Rathbone (a.k.a. Ratbone) was well read and had been one of the few Dry Creek Gulchians interested in literature back in the old days when he'd led a successful and relatively harmless street gang, the opposite number to the Dirty Dog Gang from which the restaurant drew its name.

But he'd read all of Sage's stuff about a hundred times and had no interest in reading anything by Niemand

Kompt. With a little sigh of contentment, he turned over on the pile of blankets and pillows the Squidren had thoughtfully provided in this dark corner, and prepared to take a nap.

The droning of their not-so-fascinating literary discussion would probably help him sleep.

One more thing of importance happened during the time that Ratbone slept and the two authors, much to their surprise, were enjoying their discussion and discovering that they actually had a lot in common.

Since their worldviews were and always had been diametrically opposed, it was fascinating to discover that they were actually mirror images of each other. Fitting their minds together like two halves of a plastic egg somehow gave a complete picture of the range of attitudes humans could take towards each other and their universe. Fate, love, power, life and death, faith and cynicism, all that and everything else were contained within this egg.

Great depths were here, and also the manifold ways that good and evil might hide inside each other, like the dots of light and dark in the centers of the two halves of the Tao symbol.

Ratbone woke briefly at this point and lodged an objection to the constant, boring, and incredibly harmful equating of light and dark with good and evil to which so-called western civilization was so addicted.

When he realized that neither of the others thought this way, not even Neimand Kompt, and heard a few famous quotes about the depth and beauty of the Dark, he turned over and went peacefully back to sleep.

Actually, the really important thing happened right at a moment when all three were riveted on their discussion, so all of them missed it.

Suddenly a harsh and intrusive voice called out, "YOU'RE *UNDER ARREST!*" This was followed by faint murmurs of protest, polite Squidish objections, and finally by a loud cry of, "HOW *DARE YOU? I WON'T! LET ME GO!*

There was a bit more yelling, first clear and then muffled, followed by the sounds of thrashing tentacles and then of the SquidShips' hatch opening and closing.

And that was all.

CHAPTER FORTY-EIGHT

THE REAL DEFENDANT

ame spit, different day, thought the court reporter. But this time she was wrong.

JUDGE: Now, as to the more serious issue of jurisdiction, Counsel, where is the Defendant domiciled?

PUPPY: Well, that's rather a question, Your Honor. As far as the Earth Plane goes, Defendant lives in Dry Creek Gulch, Squid Protection Zone, Southwest U.S., Planet Earth. If this were her only or even original identity, the jurisdiction would clearly be with either the human or the Squidish authorities overseeing that area.

JUDGE: Does anybody know which?

PUPPY: No, Your Honor. That's one of the problems.

JUDGE: Proceed.

A SQUID: Your Honor, Magbatz Blaghblatz representing the Squid Planet. The defendant was a Squid long before she was human. Her Squidish identity is controlling because it is both prior and more important. The Squidren clearly outrank the Earthbound humans in every possible way. Also, *she is actually a Squid—*

JUDGE (interrupting): Well, that seems clear enough. Defendant will be treated as a Squid, one who has assumed a temporary Earth identity.

NEW VOICE: Just a minute, Your Honor. Her Squidly identity is *also* a constructed identity rather than an original one. Defendant is actually an [unpronounceable combination of sounds, lights, other types of high-frequency vibrations, and things that cannot be put in human terms at all.]

MORE VOICES: *STOP!*

This chorus of voices could be described as chiming, resonant, ringing, or synchronous but slightly out of phase. The authority in them supersedes everything and everyone in the room, including the Judge. All others fall silent.

SHE IS MORE THAN THIS.
TRULY, SHE IS MORE THAN THIS.

After an inexplicable pause, a kind of timeless time, the discussion resumes as though nothing has happened.

JUDGE: Having settled the issue of Defendant's name for the purposes of this trial, we return to the matter of jurisdiction. Mr. Lumpkin, are you now maintaining that this Court *does* have jurisdiction over the defendant?

F. ATTY. LUMPKIN: Yes, Your Honor. My research conducted during the recent break indicates that this is the proper venue.

PUPPY: Your Honor. In justice to my client, I must protest—

JUDGE: Yes, well, I understand some of the issues. I'm not sure the two of *you* do, however. Let me enumerate, and if you feel I've left anything out, you may address the Court.

The judge begins, emphasizing each point by extending one finger of his hands ... Well, "fingers" and "hands" are not exactly the right words ...

PUPPY: We know the issues—

JUDGE: Mr. *Puppy*! *Sit!*

(Puppy sits. So does Fatty, both from courtesy and from canny prosecutorial calculation.)

JUDGE: One. The incidents in question being scattered through time and space, particularly time, jurisdiction remains unclear. For the record, please confirm once again exactly who has the authority to adjudicate this matter?

FATTY: You do, Your Honor. There is no higher authority in the Multiverse that we have been able to discover or contact than yourself.

JUDGE: Two. Are you really sure that a trial with the opposing sides *being represented by a dog and a cat* can have anything other than an overly adversarial outcome? Will the two of you be able to resist attacking each other with more than words, precedents, and brilliant legal arguments? Because I will have no brawling in my courtroom!

FATTY: (rising): Sire—excuse me, Your Honor—you need have no concerns of this type. I believe I speak for Mr. Puppy as well as myself in saying that we take our responsibilities to the Law and the fair and impartial adjudication thereof with a degree of seriousness which precludes any difficulty based on our cultures, genders, different abilities positive or negative, time-space affiliations or, most particularly in this case, our species. *Specieses.*

With a slight bow to the Court, Fatty resumes his seat.

PUPPY (rising): While overlooking my Friend's possibly hurtful allusion to different abilities—we are all as we are made, Your Honor, and cannot help our unusual talents or deficits—I must address the matter of our differing and sometimes adversarial species affiliations. It is certainly possible, as my Friend pointed out, for us as legal professionals to rise above such petty rivalries. The law itself takes precedence. Why you yourself, Your Honor—

JUDGE: Be *careful*, Mr. Puppy, you are approaching a line that should not be crossed.

PUPPY (obstinately persisting): Your Honor, I must insist. It is manifestly unfair of you to assume, gratuitously, that my Friend and I cannot rise above our species affiliations, when you *yourself*, the arbiter of justice, are—

JUDGE: My Puppy, *stand down!* One more word and I will hold you in contempt!

Puppy reluctantly sits. The judge, his enormous body floating in his magnificent tank, waves his flippers in irritation and dismissal of Puppy's impudence. This generates an enormous wave which threatens to overflow the tank and swamp or even drown the air-breathers.

JUDGE: Council, you may proceed. Call your first witness.

PUPPY: Your Honor, I call my client to the stand.

JUDGE: Would you like to tell us her *name*, Counselor?

And for just that moment, he sounded a little like the sarcastic judge who had given Puppy such trouble previously, causing the final meltdown of his fictional character.

PUPPY: Apologies, Your Honor. I call Jennifer Preisczech, Squid Empress of the Greater Universe, to the stand.

An audible gasp arose from the throats of everyone in the courtroom. (Everyone who *had* throats, that is. As one deeply troubled alien Squid has complained so frequently, this taken-for-granted anatomical feature is not shared by everyone.)

This synchronized inhale of astonishment was followed by a communal *exhale* that created quite a wind, ruffling papers on the long tables of the prosecution and the defense. After that there was only a shocked silence.

FATTY (choking): *The Squid Empress?* Your client, the Defendant, is *the Squid Empress??*

He stared in astonishment at opposing counsel, then at the judge, and then his gaze swept the entire courtroom as he turned a full circle, trying to find a pair of eyes that held some glimmer of comprehension. But there was none. The faces from many galaxies all looked blank, dazed, and in shock. A few of the beings had fainted dead away.

At this point, the redoubtable and normally unflappable attorney F. Atty. Lumpkin, Esq. began running backwards across the polished courtroom floor in the classic maneuver of a cat about to lose his lunch. It was not until he reached the wide expanse of carpet at the back of the courtroom that he began emitting the classic choking and gagging sounds so familiar to all who share their domiciles with these magnificent creatures.

And as we all know, those of us who have that honor, no cat will throw up on a polished floor if a carpet is available.

"I believe the Prosecution rests," said Edwin Puppy firmly, his voice ringing with a confidence quite unlike his usual shy demeanor.

For something had happened to Edwin Puppy, in fact to both of him. Through their monumental struggles and their courage in confronting each strange new challenge, or perhaps through a sudden attack of the SUX^2BU technology, which was spreading like a virus through the Multiverse, Edwin Puppy and Edward Youngdog had become one.

From the back of the room came a catly voice.

"Your Honor, in view of this unexpected development, the Multiverse hereby withdraws the charges against Jennifer Preisczech, Squid Empress of the Greater Universe."

And having made this monumental effort at professional conduct, the cat returned to his choking and gagging, disgusting sounds to most, but music to the ears of the newly minted Edwin-Edward Puppy-Youngdog, Esq.

"Madam Squid Empress," inquired Judge Rumblethunder politely, "may I escort you home?"

"Thank you, Your Honor," said Jenny, appearing simultaneously as a lovely woman of Earth and a stunning electric blue Squidress. "That would be most kind of you. I would like to return to the SquidShip."

"Case dismissed," said the judge, and in the twinkling of an eye, the two of them were gone.

CHAPTER FORTY-NINE

BACK ON THE SQUIDSHIP (SMALL FIXES)

"**N**ow as we face the ultimate test of our civilization and all that we hold dear," continued the ranting voice, still going on after all this time, "it is needful to return to our core principals. The colors acceptable to right-thinking Squidren are the Red, the Yellow, the Green, the Blue, and the Black, the traditional five colors of the Braided Thread! These are clearly elucidated in *The Book of Lighted Squid!* And these *only!*"

SECOND VOICE: You mean *The Book of Squidly Light!*
FIRST VOICE: I *don't.* You are an ignorant young upstart—
    are you even five hundred years old? Or even three?
    You're a baby, and furthermore, you're a heretic! There
    is no *Book of Squidly Light!*

SECOND VOICE: There is! I have it right here (holding up a book)!

FIRST VOICE (dripping contempt): That is a stupid *novel* from Planet *Earth*.

SECOND VOICE: It's not, it's our *Holy Book! You're* the heretic! You're a *fanatic!*

FIRST VOICE: If you think *that*, you are not a true *LightSquidian!* For thousands of generations—

SECOND VOICE: *You're* not a *LightSquidian*, you're an *idiot!* The *Book of Lighted Squid* sounds like a barbecue! In fact—

It was a dangerous moment. The thousands of suddenly assembled Squidren appeared hypnotized, swaying as if at a cliff edge under the spell and assurance of these powerful speakers. If they toppled over, there would be a chain reaction leading to a Squid Rebellion or worse. The whole project would go down in darkness, perhaps taking with it the entire Multiverse.

Then a voice came ringing, the hypnotic baritone that had once swayed millions, the final authority on every sticky issue. He raised his great flippers like one about to conduct an orchestra. Then deliberately, with studied theatricality, he dropped them again.

Judge Rumblethunder, the Adequately Magnificent Presence, held their attention, then gestured politely to someone standing beside him. She walked to the podium.

"Get over yourself, *Squid!*" said the casually disgusted voice of Jenny the Squid Empress.

"I know all these high vibration colors seem a little weird to you and I get it, they seem a little strange to others of us too. But to tell you the truth, to many of your fellow beings, *you look kind of weird yourself.*

And this brief remark was made with such assurance and inner power that the officious Squid deflated like a balloon with the air let out, crumpled like a crushed paper bag. The Zi began to dance, probably from relief, and others joined them. Still others broke into laughing little conversational groups, nibbling the delicious foods that were being passed around.

Because what she said was true. Every grouping and individual from the wider Multiverse right down to any two or three individuals interacting together thought the other ones were *really weird*. And most of them still managed to be polite about it, getting the work done and having some fun along the way.

What mattered most was not how many heads you had or what color you were or exactly whom you loved, but whether you manifested courtesy, kindness, insight, courage, and intelligence. Because everybody looks really weird to somebody!

CHAPTER FIFTY

A WHILE LATER

"Where *were* you? What *happened* to you?" begged the original SquidSquad, the team that had come together to save the Earth so long ago. Unlike others on the ship who had been sleeping or distracted, they had heard the wild cries and thrashing tentacles and had suspected that the abductee was their own beloved Squid Empress.

Now they were all growing calmer, gathered round her in the comforting new lounge and observatory adjoining the SquidPool. After the bewildering colors of hyperspace, the view of a million stars laid out like diamonds on midnight-colored velvet was breathtaking.

Others quietly joined them. Sage and Ratbone and Rupert Griffin were there, as was the black labrador Sonar, whom Sage had rescued from Griffin's book *Novel* way back in the Squidly Light days. No-Name Stupid was there and an apparently recovered Fatty Lumpkin, purring on the lap of Leila Umm Nuri, who had felt a bit guilty about turning down Edwin Puppy's request and had just teleported in. Everyone was there who needed to be.

Miss O'Connell / Squidress Four appeared with the usual coffee, tea, bowls of light, bugs in seaweed, and also some tiny lemon pies and began serving them, assisted by Emma. The other three members of her catering team were obviously busy: Leila was cuddling the cat, and Jenny was the center of attention.

And from out of nowhere stepped the third caterer, Alexander Lazlo Buddy Macadamian Preisczech, magnificently dressed in a deep blue suit and white cravat, a sharp contrast to the dull greens, browns, and grays he had formerly worn. And he took Jenny in his arms right there in front of Judge Rumblethunder and everybody, and set her on his lap. They stayed that way all the time that she was telling everyone her story.

"What happened to you?" asked the Commander again, more quietly.

"I don't know," answered Jenny thoughtfully. "I was in my human form and half asleep, and suddenly all these people grabbed me. My Alex, you know, my Earth guy," she added, smiling at Preisczech, "Well, he invented something that made each of the split-off selves merge back into their one original form. But it's not quite stable yet, and it was spreading like a virus. A *good* one, though," she added hastily, not wanting to hurt his feelings.

"I caught it," she added.

As she told them the rest, they looked at her in wonder, as though seeing her for the first time. For Jenny was still Jenny, Squid Empress and ruler over a substantial portion of the Multiverse, but now she was somehow even more. Because due to Preisczech's SUX^{2}BU technology, Jenny had merged with her alternate selves.

They'd had a little trouble at first shaking down into a comfortable personality, but the transition was now going smoothly. Luckily there'd been only three of them: Olivia Squidlight, newly elected representative to the Tripartite Confederacy from the far, far future; Jenny herself in all her manifestations; and Deandra Hollendaise, blocked and thwarted by a bad upbringing and exposure to terrible values, but now free and beginning to awaken in a new way in the company of her other selves.

"When we talked about it," Jenny continued, "he told me it would be good for the three of us to merge back into one. And the process was still going on when those goons grabbed me, that's why they were *able* to. I was like a butterfly halfway out of the chrysalis."

"Who were they? And why did they take you?" asked the baffled Commander Kennedy. "Were you tesarged with anything? Did they tell you what you'd done wrong?"

"I have no idea," said Jenny thoughtfully. "They didn't say. They were big and scary, all in black with their faces covered. They didn't have badges and they didn't show a warrant or anything, they just grabbed me."

She'd been around Earth long enough to have some vague idea of its criminal and legal procedures. She knew that people being arrested were supposed to be told the reason, even supposed to be shown some official papers.

"I'm alright now, I'm back safe and sound," she said, hoping to reassure her anxious subjects and friends. "I just hope they don't do this to *anybody else!*"

CHAPTER FIFTY-ONE

AN INTERVENTION

We see that we have gotten a bit ahead of ourselves, or behind ourselves, or beside ourselves, any of which can happen to those unmoored in time and space, becoming what some unidentified Sci-Fi writer called timeloose.

You've observed and listened to Alexander Lazlo Flintstone Buddy Macadamian Preisczech tell our author and protagonist Halycon Sage that of the many inventions and innovations occurring in the Multiverse between 2024 EarthTime and the infinitely far future of Olivia Squidlight and the Council of Twelve, only two are important for our purposes: SwitchingUp™ and SUX²BU.

We've also implied that Preisczech's activation of the second technology, his own invention which collapsed multiple selves back into one, had gotten him sued by practically all of the lawyers in the Multiverse for ruining all those lovely disputes over property and copyright and inheritance and who's married to whom, and so on.

It had also precipitated the merging of Jenny the Squid Empress with her two alternate selves, Olivia Squidlight and Deandra Hollandaise, and of the shy Edwin Puppy and the assertive Edward Youngdog, who merged into one exceptionally well-rounded being.

So, now we move on to what happened with SwitchingUp™.

Do you remember that earlier in this narrative, two ancestors of Imaginary Author Karima and her Imaginary Husband, to wit, her father and his mother, had declared in the strongest terms that what was happening to Gaza was *not acceptable?* That his, "That'll do," and her, "That won't do," though grammatically opposite, meant the same thing?

And you should know that, however measured and calm these statements might have seemed, they implied the total elimination of whatever abysmally stupid and criminally cruel and destuctive behavior was destroying Gaza and related areas.

So, his mother and her father buried the hatchet in respect to his attempt to flirt with her at their children's wedding.

EDITORS' NOTE: If you've never seen a charming and handsome Nevada attorney trying to politely flirt with a deeply monogamous Midwestern wife, both being of prodigious intelligence but with entirely opposite value systems, you have *not* seen anything funny. To him, this was an ordinary courtesy he owed to *all* pretty women, while she looked at him as if he were a two-headed Squid.

So, this pair of in-laws went forth through time and space (we told you they were smart), encountered Olivia Squidlight or someone else from the far future, or maybe even Preisczech in the increasingly less imaginary Dry Creek Gulch, and acquired the SwitchingUp™ technology. And they used this on every nation that facilitated or ignored the ongoing and creeping genocide in Gaza, the West Bank, and elsewhere in the so-called Middle East and even far beyond. A few rare countries, Ireland and Yemen for instance, were not surprised.

Remember, the effects of SwitchingUp™ last only a minute and 37 seconds, but those effects are instantly shattering and life-changing.

And when they truly understood what they had done or supported or simply ignored, all the citizens, soldiers, politicians, and everyone else within these societies broke down sobbing uncontrollably just like Judge Rumblethunder, the Adequately Magnificent Presence. And after that, since everyone now felt exactly the way

Sage, Ruby, and scholars and resisters all over the world had felt all along, the so-called war was over.

The barriers opened, electricity returned, and clean water, healthy food, and medical supplies came pouring in. Under the direction of surviving and returning Palestinians, those with useful skills came in to help. Others stayed away but sent money, messages and prayers.

Over time, the rubble was cleared, the poisons removed, and the countless dead beneath it memorialized. The dead themselves could not be compensated except in Paradise (where they *were, gloriously!*), but they were honored and loved, their memories respected and redeemed.

Over decades, hospitals and homes, schools and universities, restaurants and souks and libraries, mosques and churches, all were rebuilt, as was everything else. Art treasures and glorious buildings were recreated as far as possible. Groves and crops were replanted, though the loss of thousand-year-old trees was real, as was the loss of beloved and treasured domestic and agricultural animals. (Some believe we'll see them again in Paradise.)

Though recovery would be slow and tortuous, the wars had finally stopped—all of them, here and elsewhere. The new empathy technology had opened hearts and minds to many issues. *How can I help somewhere?* thought many people who'd never before considered such a thing. The healing had begun.

<u>**MESSAGE FROM A PASSING SQUID**</u>: You know my people love to dot all the eyes and cross all the teas—and we know that you *humans* sometimes cross your eyes and golf your tees, but that is neither here nor there. We just had to give a shout-out to the brave and brilliant Jewish scholars and other Jews around the world who say, "Never again for *anyone!*" The beings of the Multiverse bow to you, even the sarcastic Chilideans.

CHAPTER FIFTY-TWO

CHAOS IN THE COURT AND WHAT FOLLOWED

J ust as it seemed that everything had gotten back to normal in the Highest Court Anywhere—well, as normal as things ever got—all the craziness broke out again.

Suddenly the room was full of appellants and petitioners, prosecutors and defenders, criminals and injured citizens and the falsely accused, nosy neighbors who had seen something, clever and interesting expert witnesses and stupid, boring ones. Everyone was ranting or babbling, urging or beseeching, aggressively arguing or smoothly persuading, all at the top of their lungs, all trying to be heard over the rest of the mob.

All the cases in the Multiverse had suddenly landed here: *Squid vs. Squid* and *Puppy vs. Redborne, Sage vs. Vargas* and *Vargas vs. Sage*; *Squids with Hurt Feelings vs. Perennially Sarcastic Chillidians; Second Chillidian Head vs. First Head and Discriminatory Squidren; Multiverse Lawyers' Guild vs. Alexander Lazlo Flintstone Buddy Macadamian Preisczech.*

And, of course, there was *Snrrr vs. Snrrrrrr* with all possible variations, hundreds of them, since the bone of contention in the cases was the vital matter of how the Snrrrr's name should actually be *spelled.*

The confusion, the running around, the madness, the interruptions, the blending and melding and interweaving and interference between the different cases and even other *court rooms*, all with shouting lawyers and bailiffs, gavel-banging judges, clamoring reporters with five or ten or a thousand arms or *no* arms, all waving their equivalent of pens and bits of paper, cameras or their equivalents flashing or banging or exploding or shooting toward the ceiling like mini rockets to make their deadlines, the different times and places and dimensions interfering with each other to the point that reality itself was in danger of crashing, not just the little micro worlds of Earth, both Alternative and SageWorld versions, but in a massive exploding breakdown of the whole Multiverse … it was too much! Something had to give.

"What can we do?" asked someone, a little desperate.

There came a Voice, not the Voice of God, far from it, but something from that general direction: a junior clerk perhaps. It was like the Voice that had said earlier, about Jenny:

"SHE IS MORE THAN THIS.
TRULY, SHE IS MORE THAN THIS."

That voice had temporarily stilled their chatter, and *this* one, the same or related, had ultimately brought them *here*.

To Nuri, Sage, and all who had experienced them, this sounded like the Squidish excerpts from *The Book of Squidly Light*, the alien holy book that always said exactly what you needed.

"To escape, you must transcend," said the Voice.

"We've *told* you that. You must go *up* (or down, same thing). There are many ways. And you each have a job to do, each one different.

"*Squidress Obiwan Mohammad* and *former Fifth Street Mofo Lieutenant Rap*, stop second-guessing yourselves. You both do it. Trust your first, good instincts. You are wise and strong.

"And Squidress, please start writing your book!" (This Being was evidently from a time before the shy Squidress and author became known across the Multiverse.)

"*KVB,*" she was *going* by that now, how did the Voice know? "you need to have some silence. Not too much, just a little. Then it will be alright."

"*Halycon Sage* and *Ruby Echevaria*, you have one more job to do together, and it's a big one. After that, you can relax and live your lives. Others will help.

"Oh, *Ratbone, Ratbone.*" (There was a burst of affection here.) *"Augustus T. Rathbone,* you are a *jewel* on the Hand of God!

"Niemand Kompt, with a little more confidence, you will be assured of success. *That's from a fortune cookie!"* the Voice added proudly. (The things that tickled the Divine Sense of Humor were sometimes deeply ridiculous.)

The Voice went on, but those who'd been named tuned out a little, suffused with relief and a certain lightness. When they tuned back in, they heard, *"No-Name Stupid,* we know you've been worrying about this: You will complete your mission. You will help to save the world.

"In fact, you can *all* stop worrying. You'll be given the tools you need. And you're all loved and treasured, though it might not seem that way, right down to Ahmed the Bug (who may in fact be one of Our favorites)."

Then, abruptly, it was over. The chaos of the thousand superimposed courtrooms had disappeared, and they were back in Dry Creek Gulch, just in time for the end of The Great Literary Conference.

CHAPTER FIFTY-THREE

A TRIUMPH!

We are pleased to report that, despite all the mishaps and general chaos, the conference was a great success and everyone had a wonderful time. At the very end, when their appearance was despaired of, two of the three missing authors returned, appearing suddenly on stage.

Redborne read *Puppy for the Defense*, the whole thing, and it was received with almost deafening applause. Sage followed by reading some of his favorite works, *Romance for Cat and Squid*, *Boo Radley Goes Hawaiian*, and, when begged for more as he was preparing to step down, The Dinosaur Trilogy in its entirety. (Or The Forget-About-It Trilogy; he could never make up his mind which name he liked better.)

His final reading was received, not with thunderous applause, but in a silence so deep that for a moment he worried that his audience had not liked it.

But only for a moment.

When they got their breath back, the audience exploded into laughter, applause, and congratulations. Everyone said they wanted to do it again next year, and in a moment of enthusiasm, Halycon Sage agreed.

There was one last writer who had not presented, who had, in a most uncharacteristic way, sat back and listened to everyone else. Sage felt guilty about this, and suppressing his doubts as to the wisdom of his action, he invited Neimand Kompt to take the stage.

Neimand Kompt looked out at the audience.

"Hi," he said.

And then he read his latest work.

A Friend

by Niemand Kompt

I made a friend today. It was okay. I liked it.

The End

Practically the shortest novel ever written, it was well received by the audience, who assured the author that they would like to hear more of his new work. Augustus Rathbone was particularly enthusiastic.

"Bye," said Niemand Kompt.

CHAPTER FIFTY-FOUR

RETURN

The highest states can be maintained only briefly; then we go back to our former level. But after experiencing that higher state, the default level itself is raised, though it's not always apparent right away. And this back-and-forth process continues.

Karima, from her normal state before writing / encountering this book, had asked, "How do you hold the joy and the agony, the laughter and the sorrow, all at the same time, or alternate between them, without seeming shallow or morbid, happily uncaring or completely insane?"

VOICE: You know that door that's sometimes locked, and sometimes not even visible, but then it opens a few inches and you think, "This is so easy. It was here all the time!" That door to the Other Place?

KARIMA: Yes, I know that one.
VOICE: Well, let's go through it.

Navigation setting locked. Trajectory activated.

Suddenly Karima was in Gaza, unseen, but seeing. She was watching Halycon Sage and an unknown man who was with him. There was someone with her as well, a woman by her side, also watching. Karima could not see her, but could feel her presence.

"This is the future, not the past," the woman whispered. "Remember that."

Sage was talking, and they stopped to listen.

"It looks amazing here now," said Sage to the white-robed figure beside him.

"It was so hard," came the answer. "*So hard*. But that time is over now. *Alhamdulillah*."

Sage took a moment to remember his former expectations, so horrendously violated on his previous visit. But now here they were, the pictures he had seen, the things he'd read about, a shining, living reality before his astonished eyes.

Date palms and olive groves and farms, animals grazing; colorful houses large and small; beautiful mosques and churches and museums. Universities with huge, magnificent buildings and manicured grounds, gathering places for the learned and for aspiring scholars, a campus of Al-Azhar University. Writers, artists, scientists. Shops and markets and restaurants, large and small, traditional and modern. The blue-green water and beautiful beaches of the Mediterranean, *al-bahr al-abyad al-mutawasit*, the White Middle Sea. Friends and families strolling, talking, eating, playing on the beach or in the ocean.

"Palestine is a beautiful country," remarked the Duolingo language program.

Karima thought they were done, but her unseen guide had one more thing to say.

"You should know, though, that this is only a *possible* future, though maybe a probable one. But for it to come true, there needs to be a major intervention by someone named هاليگن سايج.

Karima's Arabic was getting better, and after a moment, she understood. Yup. For Karima, it would always come down to Halycon Sage.

CHAPTER FIFTY-FIVE

THE BEGINNING

Bismillah ar-rahman ar-rahim, murmured Halycon Sage under his breath. This was something he'd picked up from Nuri and his family, meaning, "In the Name of God, the Compassionate, the Merciful." One would say it, he knew, at the beginning of things, to create an auspicious start. Or, not to *create* it because only Creator could create anything, but to do your own little part, specific and pre-ordained according to Nuri's family, to open the way.

He said it so softly that the editorial part of his mind, swift as the wind and always willing to interfere in any rumination or discussion, even the most important ones, decided it should be in *italics* like a thought, not in *quotes* like a comment. That was one problem solved anyway, though certainly not the most important one.

Shut up, shut up, shut up! thought Sage loudly at his inner editor. He was trying to save the world—really, ultimately this time—so he didn't have time for this nonsense.

Gaza was the flashpoint. In more than one timeline it led to the collapse of the whole planet. He had looked back into history trying to see when the problem started, and while he couldn't quite manage *that*, he'd found the origin of his *own* problem. And it looked as though fixing it would fix quite a lot of other things, maybe even in the so-called Middle East.

At the moment no one else was around, nobody to consult, so nothing remained but his intuition and the guidance of his mentor on the other side, the holy man who had once said yes to his inner heart, his mission, and his ultimate question without saying a word.

Certainly, the last remaining alternative for saving the world was completely ridiculous, but he had to do it, because it was the only thing left.

Sage walked toward the seashore, toward the white sand beach, now interspersed with dunes and little tufts of beach grass. He was alone there, one man trying again to save the world, this time from an unredeemable disaster. He looked to the right and the left, hoping for helpers, for friends, for some better inspiration. There was nothing.

Then there was Karima, walking toward him. They shared a hug, then melted into each other and became one being.

He looked out to sea.

The ships were there, three tall white-sailed ships, the same that had been taken for benign emissaries from the spirit world by some of the first to see them. If only they had known, if they could have armed, could have banded together, perhaps they could have done something. But realization had come too late.

Sage watched calmly as the ships drew nearer and nearer and finally anchored in the bay, far enough out that their hulls would not ground, yet near enough to send men in boats to begin landing on the shore. To begin the Discovery of America.

Once again saying *bismillah* and for the last time offering up his heart, his being, and his quest to Creator, Halycon Sage walked down the beach to the waterline and began to shout, waving his arms frantically. The people mooring the boats and stepping onto the land were close enough to hear him now. Close enough to see and hear him. He had learned the languages in which to address them *all*, the Spanish and Portuguese and others, and he already knew English.

He had recruited, merged with, or split into, the many Sages from many elsewhens so that every point of invasion could be covered. No tiny boat from Latvia or Sicily could sneak under their radar.

"PLAGUE! RUN!!! Run for your *LIVES!!!"* shouted Halycon Sage, frantically waving his arms like a semaphore of madness. *"RUN, RUN, YOU'LL ALL BE*

KILLED! YOU'LL TAKE IT BACK WITH YOU! ALL YOUR PEOPLE WILL DIE!"

Even as he did these things, Sage could not help feeling like an idiot, a hopeless idealist being crushed between the jaws of existential truth and harsh reality. Surely the ravings of one man, no matter how urgent, how desperate, or how crazy, could not turn back the genocidal tide of these approaching monsters. Surely it was not enough. What was he *doing* here?

A moment of stillness, and then Sage was not alone. A hundred other Sages shouted with him. Perhaps they had not all been needed elsewhere, and certainly Preisczech's virus has not touched them.

But even *those* numbers could not account for the uproar behind him.

Momentarily confused, he turned, and the first thing he saw was Ruby, triumphantly heading a phalanx of unified beings. Unified, but unbelievably diverse. She was mounted on No-Name Stupid, the brown and white pinto, at last fulfilling his exalted mission.

She wore leather riding boots, intricately tooled, and a garment combining armor with the most beautiful and glittering cloth, flashing with bits of mirrored glass intricately placed to reflect a myriad of actual rubies. Ruby and Stupid, coat brushed and gleaming, shone in the sun, which suddenly emerged from behind a cloud as if to bless their mission. She was a warrior queen, so welcome and so needed at this moment. And behind her was everyone else.

"PLAGUE!" shouted a million voices. *"PLAGUE, FIRE, MURDER! ALIENS!"*

The Squidren were there in their thousands, led by Commander Kennedy. The Chillidians were there, still mocking the ever-heroic and world-saving Squids, but along for the ride and adding their two-headed weirdness to the assault on the sanity of the aggressive invaders.

The Eminence was there in the guise of the enormous Judge Rumblethunder, flanked by everyone who'd beamed in from the courtroom chaos that began our last encounter with that venue. Yes, from that exact moment. So many shouting, conflicting voices, so many Snrrrr!

The Apocalypse Zombie was there; he had resumed his previously horrifying appearance. Niemand Kompt was there, looking as villainous as formerly.

"MONSTERS," they shouted, *"WE'RE THE MONSTERS!"*

"AND WE'RE GOING TO EAT YOU!" added the criminals who had precipitated the Barbecue Incident, joined by the four Squidren they had marked for a hideous death and the heroes—Abdurraheem, Preisczech, Ratbone, and another Halycon Sage—who had rescued them, shouting their slogans with roaring joy.

Jenny the Squid Empress was there still merged with Deandra and Olivia and flanked by her court ladies who had also participated in the rescue at the Attempted Barbecue.

Everyone was there—energized, furious, triumphant, and happy all at once. Perhaps the Chillidians and the Squidren were the most terrifying thing to the invading

Earthlings, who had not seen anything like them before, but one more creature put the icing on the cake.

"*MAY I HELP YOU?*" came the grating, grinding voice. There was a definite saurian look to this character, like a tyrannosaurus or allosaurus, but not entirely real looking, more like a blow-up monster from some fairground attraction or extravagant Christmas display. It opened its mouth. Its teeth were enormous, maybe six inches long for the protruding incisors that extended over its lips.

"*WELL??? WHAT CAN I DO FOR YOU??*" the thing roared, beginning to sound impatient. With both its tiny, claw-ended arms, it held something out toward the waiting ships, toward the appalled and terrified Conquistadors and Pilgrims and the other interlopers.

Vastly insignificant and ordinary in contrast to the creature presenting it, it was a small … black … plastic … entirely ordinary … AM/FM … radio.

The invaders turned and fled. It was Turtle Island again, and would be for a long, long time.

THE END

FINIS, SERIOUSLY!

Letter to Robert Grudin

Dear Professor Grudin,

Greetings, and I'll cut to the chase: It seems only right to tell you that a version of you has manifested as an important character in my second novel, *The Book of Squidly Light*, and also in this sequel, the third of a trilogy.

I sought out your novel *Book* after reviewers said I was writing metafiction, and my feelings about the dog Doppler inspired the creation of time-traveling author Rupert Griffin, the book *Novel,* and the dog Sonar. Incidentally, this saved me from the horrid fate of having a historical figure I didn't want to include at all as a major character.

Two things gave me the courage to contact you: your describing yourself on LinkedIn as a "temporary adjunct 2nd assistant associate," in your own organization, which bespeaks humility as well as humor, and the fact that *Squidly Light* was among the May 2020 recommendations in the ALA's *Booklist Magazine,* which "is read by over 60,000 librarians for use in acquiring titles for their collections."

A new edition with a better cover and new front and back matter superseded the original one, and in both editions, you are acknowledged and much appreciated. With this, the final book, the trilogy is complete. I now add my personal thanks as well, may I cornily say from the bottom of my heart?

Yours very truly,

Karima Vargas Bushnell
Assistant to the Squid Empress

ABOUT THE AUTHOR/ ACKNOWLEDGEMENTS

While I might look like a simple and slightly absurd 1970s hippy, I'm the product of many cultures, social levels, and spiritual traditions. Thanks to Swami Atmanishtananda Saraswati, Rabbi Yonassan Gershom, Shaykh Nur al-Jerrahi, Imam Bilal Hyde, and many others including my friend Sindibad, Abdul-Haqq, Eagle Horse, Charging Snail[46], who grabbed me by the shoulders, stared into my eyes, and told me, "You're a Heyoka! You do everything backwards! You can't help it!" And to my paternal grandfather and his parents, whose indigenous heritage was hidden, but whose light shines in my heart.

---

46 Only the first and last of these four names were self-bestowed